CLAIMING THEIR MATE

THE WOODLAND WOLF PACKS
BOOK TWO

AMELIA SHAW

PROLOGUE

GRAYSON

I could smell the fear rising from the woman in front of me. The scent made me want to back away, to save her from the discomfort.

But this wasn't about me, this was about my pack. My family.

I needed to speak to this human mate that Dexter's pack had found. Claire.

Dex had said I could ask some questions of Claire if I kept my distance. It was an odd request but I was willing to honor it, if it meant I might get some answers.

What was Dex worried about? I wasn't going to hurt her. He knew me better than that.

Or I thought he did.

Because if he was worried about me trying to steal Claire away from him, that was laughable. The last thing I'd do was try to take something that didn't belong to me. That wasn't my style at all.

Not that Claire the doctor wasn't pretty. She was. But I couldn't sense the animal magnetism that Dex and his pack mates, Taylor and Jay, boasted about.

To me, she didn't smell sexy. Instead, she smelled like... theirs. And my Alpha wolf didn't stir for any taken woman. Especially not one already mated to another. Or in Claire's case, with three fated mates.

Claire stepped closer to Dex's Omega, Jay, who grabbed Claire and hauled her against his body in an uncharacteristically alpha-like gesture.

I turned my face away, to try and avoid them seeing my disbelief. It was all I could do not to laugh out loud. What did Jay think I was going to do? Grab their mate, strip her down and take her in full view of everyone here?

"What are you doing, Dex?" Jay demanded, and Dexter stepped away from our group to stand by his mate once again. Dex's Beta, Taylor, quickly joined him. Claire was flanked by her three pack mates, all of them vibrating with tension.

Dexter shook his head. "Don't worry, I don't like this any more than you do."

Seriously? What was wrong with these guys? Their human mate could not possibly be that precious.

Taylor and Dexter flagged Claire, with Jay moving slightly behind, and she relaxed into them, a soft smile lighting up her face.

That smile, and the comfortable familiarity between them all, was the first sign I'd seen of a true connection between her and her mates, and it was reassuring to see. I hadn't really been sure it was real, until now. Their connection was what I wanted... what I craved. A mate. A true love. Someone who would feel like the missing part of me. Someone I would die for, if I had to.

Mary, Dexter's mom, stepped up to speak to Claire for us. She'd brokered the discussion with Dexter, raising the issue we wanted answers to, and it was due to Mary's influence that Dex had agreed—albeit reluctantly—to let us meet his mate.

"Claire, some of the neighboring packs wanted to meet you," Mary said. "I hope you don't mind?"

Claire looked us up and down from the safety of her mens' arms, and said, "Considering the lack of women in this town, I can understand the interest." She looked straight at me this time. "Hi, I'm Claire."

I was the one who needed to step up and talk on behalf of the others, obviously. "I'm Grayson."

Claire extended her hand. "An Alpha, I presume?" she asked with a raise of one delicately arched eyebrow.

I grinned in acknowledgment and heard Dex inhale sharply. What was he worried about?

"How'd you know?" I reached out and shook her hand.

After a couple of seconds of what felt like tense silence, there was a collective sigh of relief from Dex, then Taylor and Jay.

Claire shrugged and withdrew her hand. "You're big."

I fought the heat that flashed up my face and glanced down at the huge body my Alpha genes guaranteed. "Ah... you're learning our ways, I see. It's nice to meet you, Claire. May I ask you a question?"

"Of course."

I opened my mouth, and then shut it again, hesitating instead of plunging forward. How did I ask her what we needed to know? She represented a solution to our problem, but it was a solution none of us had considered, until now.

For fifty years, not a single female had been born to our pack. The elders had believed that it meant our fated mates were non-existent for our generation. A romantic myth that had ended with our parents' matings. And in that assumption, the inevitable decline of our pack had been at the forefront of everyone's minds.

But Dexter had found his mate in the human population. And even more unusual, he'd found one female for his whole pack of three wolves. Claire had turned out to be the fated mate of Dex, Taylor and Jay, and she was one hundred percent human.

Was that really the future for the other mini-packs of three men, including mine? To share a woman in such a way?

"Go on, ask me whatever you want," Claire repeated.

I sighed and just went with what was in my head. "Can you give us a hint about what to look for with our mate? Since it appears we all need to be on the hunt for a human now."

Claire tilted her head. "Well, for one thing, I wouldn't use the word hunt when you're talking to her." She grinned at me and I couldn't help grinning back.

This one had a cheeky streak. Dex and his pack would need to stay on their toes.

Claire continued. "To be honest, though, I'm not sure what to say. Did Dexter tell you about the fainting thing?"

He had... and I suddenly realized why they'd been so hesitant to have me touch her. They'd been waiting to see if Claire keeled over when we shook hands.

But we hadn't. Interesting. That meant she really was fated for Dex's triad of wolves.

"Yes," I said, after a moment. "But I was wondering if you had an idea before that? When you first saw them, maybe? I need something that I can look for in my mate, because I've met human women before and no one has ever fainted at my touch..."

Claire looked me up and down like I was a piece of meat in a butcher's case, assessing me in two seconds and somehow coming up trumps. "Maybe that's because your mate has a brain, like me, and you've been picking up tiny blondes with more boobs than anything else?"

A grin stretched across my face. I couldn't help it. So, what if I liked them easy? We only had one night each visit in town to get them into bed, and then we had to kick them straight back out again.

There was no point trying to pick up any of the decent chicks. We literally didn't have the time, nor the desire before now, to connect with humans in a long-term manner.

I was unable to resist rising to her bait. "They weren't all blonde."

My Beta, Aaron, laughed beside me, and the tension in the whole group began to relax.

Claire shrugged. "Look, I honestly don't know what to tell you. I'm a doctor who's barely dated in a decade. Maybe your mates are the same? Women who work too much and never get out—not to the places you'd usually go to find a date, anyway."

Why didn't she just ask me to find a needle in a haystack?

"Then how am I meant to find her?"

Claire bit her lip and glanced away. Then she looked back at me with a reluctant smile.

"Fate," she said. "You have to trust that you'll stumble across her when the time is right. But I wouldn't be avoiding trips to town during the day. If you guys can start going in more often, you'll have a much better chance of meeting the right one."

I looked over at my Beta and he nodded.

"Any other tips?" Brad, my Omega, asked.

Claire looked to Brad. "Well, I will tell you that I knew there was something special about Dexter the moment I saw him. My heart was pounding and I could barely breathe. I've never had a response like that to any man before and I'm sure your mates will feel the same way when they meet you."

A sense of relief filled me at her words. There was hope. I had to focus on that element. Hope that there was a mate for me. For us.

I just had to ignore the surprisingly massive mountain of doubt and worry that threatened to bury the hope.

I leaned forward and got her attention, my mind spinning with the implications of what she was saying. I needed to get a job in town. At the very least, it would bring in more money for my pack, and best-case scenario… I'd actually find our fated mate.

"Thank you, Claire."

Dex pulled her into his arms and I took that as the signal to move off.

"Thanks Mary." I nodded at Dexter's mom and gestured to my mini-pack—my Omega and Beta. "Let's go."

Fifteen years ago, the elders of our pack passed a new law. Due to the lack of females and over-abundance of male shifters in our pack, we were told to arrange ourselves in triads. We had to form our own mini-packs, with an Alpha, a Beta and an Omega to each family.

I hadn't known Aaron or Brad very well when they'd approached me to become their Alpha in a pack, but it had worked out better than we'd expected.

I'd die to save them, every day of the week. They were my family. But I also wanted my mate, and if that meant sharing her with Brad and Aaron, as Dexter had done with his pack, then I would.

Anything to have a true family, and maybe even children one day.

I hoped our mate—if she existed—would one day fulfil the aching need inside my chest that I'd had for more than a decade.

I loved the larger pack, the elders and my blood-related family. But there was a place inside my heart that was gaping wide open. Empty. Ready and waiting for a woman to love and cherish.

"So, what do you want to do?" Aaron asked me as we walked to our front door and stepped inside our too-large home.

"We need to go into town and cover as much ground as possible. I'll apply for a job and see what happens. Our mate has to be out there."

"A job? Where? On a building site full of men?" Aaron rolled his eyes and I stopped to consider his words.

He was right. We were tradies. How were we going to meet women that way?

"There're women at employment agencies. You could apply for jobs everywhere and not necessarily take any," Brad piped up, and I turned to smile at him.

My Omega was quiet, but smart as a whip.

"That's an idea. Somewhere to start, at least." I glanced at my watch. It was only one p.m. There was still plenty of daylight left, to begin the process of looking.

"I'll go and ask some of the elders if they need anything from town. Might hunt around a little now."

"I'll go with you," Aaron said, his mouth setting with determination.

Brad shrugged. "I've got work to do here. Let me know how you go."

Aaron and I headed to the elders, but it seemed they needed nothing today. Then we jumped in the car and drove to town, a strange vibration of excitement rattling through me. I could tell from the way Aaron held himself, that he was feeling the same kind of strung-out anticipation, too.

When we arrived in Little River, I looked around with fresh eyes.

The air was cleaner, crisper and better than it had been the last time I'd been there. The colors were brighter and the sounds around me happier.

I knew it must be all in my imagination, but how could I not be feeling more positive after the chat with Claire? There was a chance that we could meet our mate, and soon.

"Should we split up and try different places?" Aaron asked, clearly struggling to hide his own smile.

Women walked by us, their gazes skimming over our bodies and some of them sending subtle invitations with their eyes.

I knew that humans were attracted to us. They liked muscles, of which we had an abundance.

It didn't mean much in the pack. Everyone was strong, hard-working and super-fit.

But in this world, where people worked while sitting in a chair all day, the men were not as strong, healthy, or trim.

"Yeah, why not," I said in answer to Aaron's query. "We could walk around and see if anyone faints at our feet." I grinned at Aaron, and he laughed.

The hunt was on.

I glanced around at a pair of women walking up the street, their long, straight hair billowing around their faces, their too-skinny legs wrapped in thin skirts.

I inhaled deeply, hoping to smell something new, sweet, and distinct.

But there was nothing except the normal scents of the city. The people around us offered up a range of scents, but none grabbed my attention and held it.

I went to turn away, but Aaron grabbed my arm. "Do you think we'll have a different mate each? Or one to share like Dex's pack?"

I shrugged. "No idea. Doesn't really matter, either way, does it?"

"Guess not." He sounded a little uncertain. Then he added, "You don't care?"

I stared at him, surprised by his question. "Of course, not. After spending a decade coming to terms with our shitty, one-night-stand existence, I'll do anything to find my true mate. To have a woman to come home to, and children. If she's meant for you and Brad too, then so be it."

I didn't have jealousy issues like a lot of the other Alphas.

I lived for my pack.

And if Fate had decided one human was enough for us, then I would ride that wave and be grateful for it.

"Oh, good." Aaron seemed happier now, more relaxed. "I feel the same way."

We grinned at each other, and I could read the hope in Aaron's eyes, now.

"Let's go," I said. "See you back here in two hours."

He grunted and we turned in opposite directions.

I walked along the streets and ducked into a pharmacy, a green grocer and a liquor store, making small talk with the locals, telling them I was looking for some work in housing construction.

None of the women smelled any different to me, and I shook so many hands. Everyone's hands.

They must have thought I was the politest person around.

And yet, no one fainted at my touch. Not even an offer to go out for dinner or a drink.

Not that I should have expected to find my mate on the first day. That would have been ridiculous. But as the time dragged on, my heart grew heavy. And when the designated time came and went, I forced myself back to the car, to discover Aaron's sad face.

"No luck?" I asked him, though the question was barely necessary. His slumped shoulders and the defeated set to his jaw made the answer too apparent.

"No. Although I inquired at a job recruitment agency and they said they'd call in regards to an interview... or something like that. I wasn't really listening, to be honest."

We got in the car and I turned the key. I was surprised by the amount of disappointment running through my blood. It felt like a cancer, insidious and potent.

I forced out a laugh, trying to lighten the mood. "After a

decade of thinking we had no fated mate, we shouldn't expect her to just turn up on our doorstep in the first hour, right?"

Aaron nodded, then stared out the window and didn't say anything else.

Mopey bastard.

I sighed and turned the car back toward the pack.

Despite my conscious efforts to stay positive and grateful, Aaron's shitty attitude pretty much summed up how I felt, too.

We'd waited long enough.

I didn't want to wait any longer.

It was our time to find our mate. To begin our life. To finally be a true family. Because, without a woman or children, we were nothing.

1

NEVAEH

A month later

"Seriously, Claire. Why on earth would you choose to move all the way out here?"

My old car bumbled along the dirt road that led into some sort of secret compound that no-one knew about.

Not even Google could find the address when I plugged it in. If Claire hadn't left me hand-written instructions at the hospital, I would never have found the place.

That should have been my first hint that something dodgy was going on.

"Oh... There they are."

Houses began to appear out of nowhere, on properties cut into the hill side. Well-made, large homes sitting on big plots of land.

I glanced at the sheet of paper from Claire for the thousandth time.

First house on the left.

Number seven.

Double story with my new black truck parked around the back.

I looked up at the house to my left.

Yep. Looks like the right one.

I pulled up into the area at the front of the house—I couldn't really call it a driveway—and got out of the car.

The roads weren't that wide and the lack of driveways made no sense. Did everyone park around the back? Or did most people from this town walk everywhere?

"She's lured me out here to la-la land."

I admired Claire more than any woman I'd ever known. She was easily the most driven, accomplished female physician I'd ever met, but she'd changed somehow in the past month or so. People at work thought it was due to her breaking her arm during the attack at the hospital, but I had another theory.

I had a feeling it had everything to do with the man she'd moved out here for. And I was here to find out if I was right.

They said men made women soft... or was it the other way around? I couldn't remember. I spent too much of my time working and staying away from those of the other gender, so I wasn't sure what they were or weren't.

Didn't matter. I wasn't hooking up with anyone of any gender, anytime soon.

I clutched my bag to my side and kept my keys in my hand, just in case. In case of what, I wasn't sure. But that was my instinctive reaction as a small female in an unknown town.

Movement caught my eye and I turned to see three men step onto the front porch of the property next door.

Three large, exceptionally well-built, gorgeous men.

The effect on my body was embarrassing.

I couldn't breathe and my heart began to gallop, pounding against my rib cage in an unending way.

What was wrong with me?

I locked eyes with the largest one of the three and heat poured through my belly and worse, lower still.

The other two turned to stare at me. My knees buckled under what felt like the weight of the three combined gazes, and I stumbled forward.

No. No. This wasn't happening.

I ran for the front door of what I prayed was actually Claire's house, and banged on the wooden panels.

Somehow, I could still feel the men next door staring at me, the sensation making the hairs on my neck stand up.

I couldn't stop myself from looking across to them once again. They stood in their jeans and tank tops, their muscles bulging out of their arms and shoulders.

None of them were my sort of men... not at all.

Fear skittled along my spine at my own inexplicable reaction, and I called out.

"Claire!"

The front door swung open and there was Claire in the doorway, her arm still in a full cast past her elbow.

"Nevaeh! You made it."

I launched myself at my friend and shut the door behind me.

My heart was still pounding and I couldn't quite catch my breath, but I was finally safe inside Claire's home.

"Nevaeh, are you okay?"

"Yes, yes. Just ran here from the car."

To get away from the sexy trio next door.

I looked at my friend and was blinded by the glow of good health surrounding the woman who had once worked a hundred hours a week.

Whatever Claire was doing out here certainly agreed with her.

"Doctor Claire Monaghan," I addressed her in a mock-stern tone. "What are you doing this far out of town?"

She grinned. "Enjoying the fresh air."

I glanced around the well-made house, noting the carved staircase and a hand-made table that drew my eye. I could see Claire's touch everywhere, too. From the colorful pillows on the sofa, to the lemons arranged in a glass bowl on the kitchen counter.

"Wow. This is a really beautiful house, Claire. Elegant but still homely at the same time. It must be nice to have so much space."

Like most shift workers who lived in town, I shared a two-bedroom apartment. In my case, my room-mate was another hospital nurse. Our space was cramped and old, but it was home. A place to rest my head at the end of a shift.

My apartment had nothing on this place.

"Oh, yeah, thanks. The boys built the whole house together. I've just added a few touches to make it more homey. I want to get a huge sofa so we can all sit together, but that hasn't happened yet."

She pointed to her arm, as though that was the reason she hadn't been shopping.

But my head was stuck on her phrasing. The boys?

"Um... what do you mean by that, exactly? I thought you moved out here to live with your boyfriend? Does he have house-mates, or something?"

I looked around as though the house would give me a clue as to what she'd meant, but there were no signs of anyone. And no photos, either.

"Ah, yeah. Sort of."

Claire's face was doing something I hadn't seen before. It was turning red, and if I used my nursing intuition, she looked like she was lying or hiding something. That was a look I'd seen on many patients' faces, but had never seen on this doctor's face before.

"Claire." I frowned my confusion. "What's going on?"

She clapped her good hand to her face as if aware how heavily she had blushed, and laughed softly. "I've gotta get better at lying."

Now she had my interest.

"What are you lying about? Why you're here? Or about your guy?"

Claire's gaze slid sideways and she bit her lip. "Kind of both."

My stomach tightened with foreboding. An instinct I didn't ignore. Did it have something to do with the guys next door? I hoped not... but I couldn't discount anything at the moment.

"What's happened, Claire? What is this place? Are you in danger?"

I had a nose for bad guys now. Maybe this had something to do with the men I'd seen outside. Especially the really big one. In my experience, they were always cruel.

Claire's laugh shattered my tight stomach. "Oh, God, no. These men would die to protect me. It's not that... it's just... I'm not dating one of them... Seriously, I can't believe I'm saying this aloud finally." She paused and a small, strange giggle emerged before she said, "I'm dating all three of the men who live here."

Shock rippled through me. I felt it first in my face, which stiffened into what I know must have been a horrified expression. Then the shock traveled through the rest of me, like a cold lake, freezing each of my muscles, one at a time.

I slumped against the back of my chair and let my gaze drop to the ground. Three boyfriends? And they all lived here together? How was that even possible?

This woman was my idol. Now she was some sort of... what? I was afraid to even think anything critical in relation to Claire.

"Nevaeh, look at me."

I pulled my gaze up, to where Claire was sitting forward on her chair. Her eyes, and her tone were beseeching.

"Don't look at me like that, please. You have to understand, it just kind of happened."

Seriously? That echoed in my head like the excuse every pregnant teenage girl ever said.

"How does something like that just happen, Claire?"

I could hear my tone and it was angry, and I couldn't work out why. This was Claire's life, not mine, and I had no right to judge her decision-making.

There was a tingle of something akin to adrenaline in my veins, so I stood up and began to pace the room so that I didn't start to twitch.

"It... that doesn't make any sense, Claire."

Her eyebrows snapped up. "Hey! It's not you that needs to sleep with three men at once. I do, and I love it, not that you asked how I feel it about the situation. So, what's gotten into you? I thought you'd be happy for me!"

I whirled at Claire's angry voice. "I am!"

It was an automatic response and not at all true, and both of us knew it.

Claire's gaze narrowed. "You're lying, and I think you need to work out what's going on with you, because this is not about me."

I threw myself back down onto the couch, embarrassed by my hissy fit, tears in my eyes. I could barely even explain it to myself, let alone Claire. "I thought you were like me," I began. "You know..."

"No, I don't know what you mean. In what way?"

"Married to your job. Single. You know... not into men."

Claire's eyes opened wide. "Oh, I'm not gay... is that what this is about? Because I'm sorry if you thought..."

That snapped me out of my doldrums, double time. "Oh, no. No! I'm not a lesbian or anything, it's just..."

Claire was the job, as I was. Or she had been, until now. There was nothing else in my life that I relied on except my work.

I heaved a sigh. I didn't know why I was being so rude. I dashed away the tears on my face and took a deep breath.

"Let's start this again. Hi, Claire. You look amazing. Obviously living in the woods and not working agrees with you. Your skin is glowing!"

Words I never thought I'd say, but there they were. Out in the open. And these words, I meant.

Claire smiled and her eyes went suspiciously glossy. "I'm pregnant."

To who?

"That's brilliant... are you happy about it?" I didn't know how else to ask.

Claire coughed over her laughter and tears slid down her face.

I rushed over to her couch and took her hand in mine. "I'm so sorry for being such a wreck. You know me and my issues. I didn't mean to push them all on you."

Claire laughed properly this time, and wiped at her tears. "Oh, I'm not sad. Don't worry, just emotional. Bloody hormones."

Well, at least it wasn't my fault. I couldn't stand the idea of causing Claire harm. "So, you're... happy about the pregnancy, then?"

Claire turned to me and squeezed the hand she held. "Yes, definitely. Look, as far as the world is concerned, I'm dating Taylor. Dexter and Jay are just our housemates. But as my friend, I wanted to be honest with you. I love them all, and they love me, which... you will see soon enough, because I think I hear them coming."

I jumped up and ran across the room to my previous seat as the door banged open and a flurry of testosterone and muscles came in the door.

I looked for the men I'd seen this morning, but they were

nowhere to be seen, and amazingly I recognized a twinge of disappointment inside of me.

"Hey, baby, what's wrong? You okay?" one of them asked, his concern obvious as he moved toward Claire.

There were three of them, just as Claire had said. Small, medium and large.

The small one went straight to Claire's side and cupped her face to look at her tears.

She nodded. "Yeah, I'm okay. You know what I'm like at the moment."

The small one smiled and dropped a tender kiss on her lips. "I do."

Then he looked up and saw me. "Oh! You said you had a friend dropping in. Hey, I'm Jay."

The guy, who had a big happy smile and spiky hair, made me instantly comfortable and at home in this house.

How he did that, I had no idea, but I was grateful for his warmth.

"Hi, I'm Nevaeh. I'm a nurse at the hospital."

The other two men approached and their strength pushed through the room as though they'd reached out and touched me.

I pulled my legs up and hugged my knees into my chest.

Medium and large kissed Claire too, their touches on her face and neck both possessive and caring. Despite my earlier reservations, I was transfixed watching them all.

I didn't dare blink in case I missed something, and yet my belly tightened. And it wasn't with fear. These men were kind of... hot. The whole situation was kind of sexy, in a hugely taboo way.

I began to think about some of the advantages to Claire's system. She'd get three times the kisses, the affection, the time and the effort.

Though in my case, it could just as likely be three times the vicious attacks and stalker-type behavior.

I shuddered as my thoughts turned dark.

"I'm Taylor," the medium one introduced as he sat beside Claire and casually pulled her onto his lap.

"Dexter," the big one said, crossing his arms over his chest. My throat thickened and I swallowed awkwardly.

He was as big as a wrestler.

Claire reached up and patted Dexter's big, beefy arms. "I know he's huge, but he's a massive teddy bear. Don't be stressed by him. He works his ass off building houses every day. Don't you, hun?"

Dexter looked down at Claire and I saw the hardness around his features fade to warmth.

Yep, in this case it was clearly the woman who made these men soft.

"Oh, I'm not scared... it's okay."

Taylor rolled his eyes from where he sat on the couch. "Really? 'Cause you smell like a rabbit about to bolt. But in this case, you probably want to run like your ass is on fire."

"I smell like it? What do you mean?"

Was I farting or something? Because it was literally impossible for humans to smell fear. Animals yes... humans, no.

Claire cleared her throat. "Ah... what he means is..."

"Would you like a hot drink or something, Nevaeh? Did I say that right?" Jay asked, getting up and moving to the open plan kitchen area.

"Ah, yeah, you did, and a coffee would be great."

"You working tonight?" Claire asked.

"Yeah. Caffeine needed. You know what it's like."

"Yeah... if you can get it by IV, then even better."

I shared a smile with my friend, my colleague. I finally began to relax.

The men must have felt it too, because the two bigger guys got up to leave.

"We gotta get back to work, but we'll see you for dinner, okay?"

They both kissed Claire, waved to me and left.

I could breathe again, and Jay brought me a strong coffee in a massive mug.

"Oh, perfect. Thank you."

He smiled. "We don't do caffeine much, but Claire loves her coffee and we made sure we bought a good machine so she could have coffee whenever she wanted."

He sat down next to her with easy confidence and wrapped an arm around her shoulders.

It made me uncomfortable, the easy affection between them.

Happy couples often had that effect on me, and I wasn't sure why.

"Hey, Jay, you okay if Nevaeh and I have an hour or so to chat?"

"Oh, yeah, cool. I've got some computer work to do. I'll just be in my room if you need me."

Jay walked away to a room off the lounge and shut the door.

"They all have their own rooms?" I asked, now far too curious for my own good.

"Sort of. They've kept their own bedrooms from before I came into the picture, but we've made the master suite our main room and we mostly sleep there together. But the men still like having their own space, and when I go back to working nights, they'll probably sleep alone then. There's a fourth bedroom for the nursery too, which is nice."

"That does sound nice, so much space."

Claire glanced around. "Yeah, I kind of forget what it was like at my tiny apartment. I need to put it on the market soon."

She was selling up? Already? That wasn't very smart. She barely knew these guys.

"You're planning on living here... forever?"

"Yeah, definitely. If I do sell the apartment, it'll be to buy a bigger place in town, though. I like the idea of having somewhere to sleep after long shifts, and I'd love to have the guys with me, too, but the apartment freaks them out, and I agree with them that a house would be better for all of us."

That was better. I didn't like the idea of Claire having nowhere to go if they broke up.

"Wow, sounds like you've got it all worked out."

Claire nodded slowly. "Yeah, we kind of do."

"What about work? Are you going to reduce your shifts, or...?"

How could she want to give up working? After so many years of study, and struggling to become the best she could be, Claire was going to give it all up, for... men?

"I'll have to come back slowly after my arm heals, and by then I may need to reduce hours because of my pregnancy, but you know... work isn't everything."

Work was everything, for both of us. Or... it had been.

I wanted to laugh, or cry—or both.

Instead, I crossed my arms over my chest and glared at the woman opposite me.

"Maybe not for you, but it still is for me, Claire."

She'd sold us out. And by us, I meant all the other single, work-minded women out there.

Claire cocked her head to the side, and I could almost see the bevy of questions whirling around in her mind.

"What's up with you, Nevaeh? Why do I get the feeling that you want to tell me something?"

"I don't know what you mean. I only came out here to visit and see how you were getting along after being away from work for so long. I kind of figured that you'd be going out of your mind with boredom."

Claire cackled with laughter. "Oh, yeah, those were the days. When my whole world revolved around work, double shifts, and patients."

She was talking about it like it was the past.

"Are you seriously going to give up your whole life for these guys?"

She pinned me with a glare this time. "I'll give up whatever I want to for love, sex and the babies I've always wanted, Nevaeh. In fact, I'm gaining a whole life, not giving one up. What is it to you?"

My face flamed with the heat of shame. Yeah, I deserved that.

"I'm sorry, Claire. I just always saw you as a woman who was kind of married to her job. Like me."

I managed to pull my gaze up and meet her eyes. I could see the anger fading, replaced by a kindness that made me want to cry again.

"What really happened to you, Nevaeh? Is it childhood stuff? Or have you been burned too many times?"

This was so not where I wanted this conversation to go.

"I think it may be time I head home."

I moved to stand up and Claire commanded, "Sit your butt back down. You're acting like a spoiled little brat, and I want to know what's going on. And if you won't tell me, I'll get Dex to sit on you until you talk, and believe me, that is two hundred and seventy pounds you don't want squishing you."

A shiver crawled up my spine and I bounced my legs up and down.

"I don't like to talk about it."

"No one does."

She waited and so did I.

Finally, the words crept out of me. "My childhood was okay. We were poor, but my parents did the best they could."

"Okay... so it's a guy, then. Is he still around?"

I shook my head. "No, I... have a restraining order on him. He was one of my first boyfriends. You know, bad boy, wrong side of the tracks, all the normal cliché things..." I laughed to cover the tension I felt talking about Trevor.

There was a tight fist in my gut that never really went away. A bone-deep fear that I'd never really be free of him.

"But he, uh... got weird, possessive, after a while. And I don't really know why, to be honest, because it's not like he loved me, or even seemed to like me, actually. But he couldn't stand me being at work."

I sniffed and grabbed for a tissue from my handbag, blowing my nose in an attempt to tell my story without crying. I hated admitting to anyone that I'd been such a bad judge of character. That in my need for love and acceptance, I'd ended up with several black eyes and a stalker instead.

"Anyway... it ended badly. I've reported him to the police, but he still stalks me. I get messages on my phone, and no matter how many times I change my cell number, or move jobs or apartments, he always finds me. I even moved interstate for a while, but he just followed me. So, I ended up coming back home in the end."

Claire's mouth dropped open. "So... let me get this straight. You don't like men, and understandably so, because your first, and probably only boyfriend was an abusive creep who still stalks you?"

I choked on my own forced laugh. "Yeah, pretty much."

"And how long ago did all this happen?"

"Um... I was nineteen. I'm twenty-three now, so about four years ago."

"And you haven't been with anyone since?"

I shook my head. There was no way I was going anywhere

near another man. Unless he proved without a shadow of a doubt, that he was perfectly trustworthy.

And I didn't know how that would be possible, because trust had been destroyed in me.

"Nope... So, I'm pretty sure I'll be alone forever, because I can't imagine any guy taking on all the baggage I come with."

Claire laughed suddenly. "Oh, sweetheart, you're too young to give up on love."

I stared at her, not sure what else to say. If my story wasn't enough to convince her that I was cursed in the game of love, I didn't know what was.

And the biggest problem was, I kind of agreed with her. I had my whole life ahead of me, and yearned to find someone to love, yet the idea of going back to that place of vulnerability gave me nightmares that haunted me right through all my waking moments.

I didn't trust myself to choose well this time.

"Maybe you're right, Claire. But for the moment, I think I'll concentrate on work, and try not to envision you with three men at once."

I shot Claire a sidelong look and waggled my eyebrows.

She giggled, actually giggled! "It's hotter than you can even imagine, my friend. Oh, speaking of which, what's happening with Dr. Ferrari and that patient who had the hots for him?"

"Oh, it's gotten so much worse since last time you were there!"

We slid into a comfortable conversation about hospital gossip and the afternoon fell away under our friendship.

2

———

AARON

*A*fter seeing that gorgeous woman a few hours ago, my world tipped on its axis. I couldn't seem to settle my racing mind, nor the racing of my heart.

Which didn't make any sense. It was just one human woman.

A friend of Claire's, probably.

We'd managed to go to work, but all three of us had been desperate to come home for lunch, unable to stay away for some reason.

Her beautiful face... it had haunted me all day.

And the way she'd run away from us had worried me. Were we really that scary to a human woman? How would we ever find a mate if that was how normal women responded to us in our natural environment?

As I stepped onto the porch and turned my head toward Claire's house, sweetness tickled my nostrils with a scent that hadn't been there before. "What's that smell?"

I put my nose in the air and took a deep inhalation of crisp, fall air—something I didn't normally do because, well, I wasn't in shifter form and it could have looked like strange behavior.

Especially if the human woman was watching.

But I did, because I couldn't help myself. There was the most incredible scent on the air. Like honey and apple cookies, comforting and yet arousing somehow.

My Alpha, Grayson, appeared beside me on the porch. "What..."

He immediately did the same thing as me—inhaling deeply until a rumble rolled through his chest. "That's our mate," he said. "Fucking hell... It's the woman we saw this morning, isn't it?"

Grayson began moving, looking around, sniffing the air. Walking toward Dex's house.

He seemed a little stunned. No doubt I sported the same expression as I followed my Alpha.

"How is that possible?" I said. "We've been looking for a month with no success, and she just suddenly turns up out of the blue? Next door. What are the odds?"

I'd been to a dozen interviews, as had Grayson. We'd scoured the streets of Little Creek, even going into town like the rest of the larger pack, frequenting bars and restaurants most nights.

I hadn't been able to find her and neither had my Alpha.

"Come here, quick!" Grayson called from the front of Dex's house.

I ran over to the small black car parked out the front.

"Smell the air here. It's her."

Grayson garbled some more words and I realized that his ability to talk had disappeared. His teeth had shifted partially and some of his fangs had descended over his bottom lip.

He was holding onto his wolf, but barely. Which was danger-ous, especially for Claire and our mate.

"Do you need to shift and run? Because if our mate is human, the last thing you want to do is scare her off."

Grayson shook his head, breathing deeply through his nose, trying to contain himself.

I wanted to go inside Dexter's house and meet our mate—the woman for whom we'd waited our whole lives. But I needed to ask Grayson a question first.

"Does she smell like your mate? Because she certainly smells like mine."

I grinned at my Alpha and he tried to do the same. Since Dexter's triad had learned that our destined mates were no longer born to the pack, but instead were humans we had to seek out, the whole pack had transformed. Mostly for the positive, except for some petty jealousies that had arisen in small pockets here and there. Some of the men were determined not to share, the Alphas in particular. They wanted their own mates.

Not our triad, though.

Brad and I had been best friends since childhood. He was an Omega, and I was a Beta, and when we learnt of the new laws that meant we had to create our own mini-pack with a male Alpha, Beta and Omega in every triad, we did our research.

Grayson was a gentle giant who put the needs of the pack first. He was the perfect Alpha for the two of us. Strong, but not an asshole.

And that's what we wanted.

Someone we'd be proud to call our family.

So, when Grayson told me that he didn't mind sharing a mate, I'd been relieved, but not surprised. It spoke to the fact that he was as magnanimous as always.

"She does smell like my mate," he confirmed. "Let's go see her then."

We stalked toward Dexter's front door. My heart was beating like a bongo drum in my chest. I could hear the roar of my blood, the thump of my racing pulse inside my ears.

Grayson stepped up to the door and knocked, hard.

I looked back at our house. Maybe we should have waited for Brad before we approached her.

The door opened and our neighbor Claire's familiar face smiled up at us.

"Hey, guys. What's up?"

I arched my neck, looking around Claire and my gaze connected with the woman sitting on the couch.

She had long brown hair and a beautifully delicate face and I had to fight not to push Claire out of the way and rush over to the visitor.

"Ah..." Grayson coughed to clear his throat and I realized he was still struggling to contain his wolf.

I jumped in. "Would you introduce us to your guest, Claire? Please?"

She studied the two of us, and I could see understanding dawning on her face. Her mouth opened and her eyebrows flew up and then lowered slowly.

"Ah, yes... are you sure?" she whispered.

I met her intense stare and nodded slowly.

"Okay, but you need to be cautious. Nevaeh is... gun shy."

I had no idea what that meant but nodded regardless.

We moved inside their house slowly, the scent of Nevaeh rising up into my nostrils and saturating them with pleasure.

God, she's beautiful.

The arch of her cheek, the blue of her eyes... she was perfection.

And she was clearly not happy we were here.

She stood up and extended to her full height, her gaze hard as flint as she stared at us.

"Hello."

Grayson glanced at me, as surprised as I was about the harsh tone of her voice and the defensiveness in her body language.

Claire jumped between us. "Nevaeh is a nurse from work,

and one of my best friends. Nevaeh, this is Grayson and Aaron. They live next door."

I didn't know what that tone or her facial expressions were trying to say. All I could feel was the electricity in the air. The hairs on my neck standing on end and my cock thick, pressing against the fly of my jeans.

I hoped to God she couldn't see it. I had black jeans on today, and hopefully the dark, thick fabric hid my arousal.

"I'm Aaron. It's nice to meet a friend of Claire's."

Grayson wasn't moving, but I was itching to touch her. To feel her skin against mine and to see if Dex had been right about our mate's response to our touch.

And if Grayson wasn't going to step up...

"We didn't mean to barge in like this and shock you." I walked forward and held out my hand.

I heard Claire's sharp intake of breath but kept my eyes focused on Nevaeh.

She didn't smile. "It's fine. I was just leaving, anyway."

She wasn't taking my hand and I shot her a smile of encouragement. "You gonna leave me hanging?"

A ghost of a smile shivered across her lips. "Sorry, I'm being rude. It's nice to meet you, too."

She took my hand and a loud gasp filled the room. Mine or hers, I wasn't sure.

The pleasure was almost painful as it filled my veins and my lungs. I couldn't escape it. I couldn't breathe.

Then she was falling and Grayson scooped her up into his arms. She shuddered violently as soon as he touched her, moaning loudly.

"What's happening to her?" I asked Claire.

The doctor shrugged. "No idea. I was the one fainting, so I don't remember much else. She's probably just responding to touching you and then her Alpha on top of that."

Nevaeh arched her back and cried out, then she passed out again, limp in Grayson's arms.

The Alpha's muscles bulged as he trembled with her.

"You want me to take her?" I asked him.

He growled a low warning at me and clung to her. It was a noise I'd never heard in my life. I backed away, my hands up in a placating gesture, and let him hold her. Pain and confusion rippled through my skin and Claire walked over and put a hand on me.

"Calm down. This is new and strange, and you need to find a way to work through this together."

I nodded and began to pace the large living room. She was right, but now that it had happened, the idea of sharing Nevaeh wasn't as easy as I'd thought. Growls were surfacing in my chest as well, and an unaccustomed anger toward my Alpha rose.

The door opened and Dexter walked in, stopping short at seeing us in his living room. Dexter and his pack were very protective of Claire, and we approached her with caution everywhere she went. On the street, in the restaurants, and in town.

We certainly never entered their home when the boys weren't here.

"What's going on, guys?" Dexter asked, his tone strangely calm.

Claire bounced over to him and grabbed him in a huge hug. "Nevaeh is their mate! Look!"

She pulled Dex a little closer to Grayson, who growled and bared his teeth.

I fell back, expecting Dexter to lash out. Two Alphas in any pack could be dangerous, which was the main reason we were forced into our own triad families. To stop as much in-fighting as possible, in a world where there was no release for the testosterone, except running, or fighting.

Until now, that is.

Instead of arcing up, Dexter's shoulders relaxed and he began to laugh. "And you thought I was crazy for wanting to protect Claire! Karma's a bitch, Grayson."

Dexter kept chuckling, moving to the kitchen and opening the refrigerator door.

I was stunned.

He was suddenly all calm?

What about us? How would Grayson and I reach calm again?

"What do we do, Dex? When will she come around?" I asked.

Dexter grabbed some food from the fridge and began making a platter. Fruit, sliced meats and chocolate.

"Claire was knocked out for over an hour when I touched her, about ten minutes with Taylor and just kinda fell against Jay. So, get comfortable, guys. She's not coming around any time soon."

He brought over the platter and kissed his mate. "Eat up, beautiful. You need it."

I looked at Claire again. Her glowing cheeks, the food her mate was shoving at her...that could only mean one thing.

"You're pregnant?"

Claire grinned at me and Dexter scooped her up and put her in his lap, sitting on the couch with her.

"Yes," she confirmed.

Grayson began to move closer and slowly sat down on the other end of the couch with Nevaeh, who hadn't stirred and whose head still lay on Grayson's chest.

"Congratulations," he managed to get out, and I could see the calm Alpha in him coming back slowly.

"It will probably help if you put her down, Gray." Dexter turned his head and called out. "Jay, you here?"

A door opened and Jay came out, rubbing his eyes like he'd been working too hard at a computer screen.

"You called? Oh, hey, guys. Didn't know you were here.

Sorry." Then he did a double-take at the sight of Nevaeh in Grayson's arms.

"It looks like Claire's nurse friend is their mate. Can Gray put her down on your bed?"

Jay's gaze bounced around the room at everyone, finally coming to rest again on Nevaeh. "Wow. What are the odds?"

Grayson growled a little again, and this time I wanted to roll my eyes. He had to know that of all the guys in the larger pack, Claire's three were not the ones who would ever want our mate. They had their own.

"Probably a good idea, Grayson," I chimed in, not sure how this was going to play out. "Or we could take her home now?"

"I think maybe you should keep her here," Claire said, standing up and walking over to Grayson. "She's pretty scared of men, and if she wakes up in your house without me, she's going to freak out. Come on, Grayson, I'll show you where to put her. You'll probably calm down once you stop touching her."

Grayson did as asked, though it was obvious from the set of his jaw that he didn't want to.

They disappeared into the room Jay had emerged from, then returned without her.

My stomach hurt, so I grabbed for some of the food in front of us.

"So, um... congratulations," I said. "That's great news. A baby for the pack will be considered a true miracle."

"Yeah, if it's only one," Claire said, eating the fruit on the platter by the handful. "I'm going to organize an ultrasound in a few weeks, but considering our relationship, I wouldn't be surprised if it's a multiple pregnancy."

"Which would be even more of a miracle," I said.

Grayson shook himself and walked to the kitchen where he grabbed a bottle of water. "I'm sorry about the... wolf crap. I don't know what came over me."

Dexter didn't even flinch. "Grab a beer, Gray. Not water. You're gonna need the extra kick."

Grayson, who didn't drink, turned back around and grabbed a beer from the fridge. "Anyone else?"

"Yeah, me." I was still shaking and my nerves were stretched tight, ready to pounce on an enemy that didn't exist.

"Not for me," Dexter said, and Jay shook his head.

Grayson handed me a beer and sat next to me, the tension between us shaky, but finally settling.

"Well, that was more intense than I expected," I said.

Jay laughed at us. "I remember it too well. It's not something that ever leaves you, really."

That didn't sound pleasant.

I looked at Claire. "What do you mean about Nevaeh not liking men?"

Fate would surely not have sent us a woman who wouldn't accept us?

Claire bit her lip. "I'm not sure I should be the one to explain that to you."

I groaned. "Oh, please, help us out a little. You know we're going to struggle as it is. We have to explain to a human that there's three of us to love and that we're wolf shifters in a world where there are no shifter women left." ·

My head was spinning with all we had to accomplish and I suddenly realized how ridiculous it might sound to someone not of our world.

I began to laugh and wasn't sure why. There may have been a slight note of hysteria in it, because Claire smiled gently. "Okay, I'll help you. But only because I know how hard it was for me to accept my mates, and I didn't have half the baggage that Nevaeh does."

Grayson and I shared a concerned look, then sat down again on the couch, opposite Claire, and waited.

My heart pounded and my stomach tightened. I grabbed my beer and chugged some down, the cold beverage soothing some of the dryness in my throat.

"Okay... well, let me preface this with the fact that I only found out about her history today. I knew Nevaeh was a bit... gun shy. She never dates, and works any shift anyone asks her to. She's really careful with her money and never goes out."

I glanced at Grayson but couldn't gauge his expression.

"And today I found out why. It's because her last boyfriend, who sounds like he was her first and only boyfriend, stalked her after they broke up."

I glanced at Grayson, not really understanding the human reference. But it sounded bad. Like she'd been treated as prey.

"Sorry, Claire, you're going to have to explain that to us. What is stalking, in the human world?"

"Oh... um. You guys probably don't do that with women. Well, if a man is obsessed with you and you break up, he may try to stay in touch, even though you don't want to. He might follow you, call you, watch you—all against your will. It's scary and makes you afraid all the time."

As a male, and as someone who'd grown up in a small town where nothing bad really ever happened, this was a foreign concept.

"Ah... okay."

I wasn't much clearer now, unfortunately.

"So, what do we do?" Grayson asked from beside me. At least he'd gotten his voice properly back again.

"You need to be patient, and take it slow with her. She's not going to jump into bed with you guys the moment you put the moves on her. If anything, she'll run—as quickly as possible."

Claire bit her lip and I waited.

"What's wrong?" Grayson prompted.

"Just remembering what happened here with Dex and the guys, with me. They asked me to stay for two days to get to know them. That really helped me accept them as my mates. You could try to do that as well, but I don't think Nevaeh will be able to. She'll fight the natural attraction she feels, because of her fear, and you won't be able to stop her from going to work. She's far too driven for that."

"Then what do we do?" I asked.

Claire was making the situation sound impossible to fix, which it wasn't. It couldn't be.

I believed in the power of Fate, and the old stories of fated mates and perfect women. I always had. Even when I'd been told that path in life wouldn't be for me, I somehow knew that somewhere, there'd be someone waiting for me.

And now I knew I'd been right.

It was Nevaeh, and she wasn't just waiting for me, she'd been waiting for us.

"Well isn't she lucky that there are three of us to look after her?"

Claire laughed, and then put a dainty hand over her mouth. "Ah, no. That's gonna work against you, I'm afraid. She was horrified when I explained about my triad."

"Shit," Grayson grunted.

"I'll second that," I said.

This was getting worse by the minute. What could we do?

I looked around the room, then stood up so I could pace. I always thought better when I was on my feet.

We needed someone to talk to her, to explain. Someone she trusted...

"Claire! You can help us. You can talk to her, explain about our ways. Vouch for us. You know we'd never hurt her."

I'd spoken to Claire practically every day since she'd moved in with Dex's pack.

Sure, I didn't come too close, nor did I venture inside her house, but she knew us. Surely, she'd help.

She looked from me to Grayson, to Dexter, and back again. "Ah... I suppose I could. I know her better than anyone, and I know how hard it is to accept this world when you've been raised as a human."

"So, you'll help us?"

Claire nodded, her eyes wide with what looked like trepidation. "Yes. I will."

"Thank you."

3

NEVAEH

What the hell were they talking about? Me?

I didn't know if anyone was in the room with me, and tried to stay still in case someone was close by. Prickling unease and fear made me hold my breath so they wouldn't know I was awake, but the pain in my chest became too great, and my breath whooshed out in a fast stream.

My eyes flickered open and I glanced around the room. I was alone.

Why was I on a bed, in a strange room?

My heart beat so loudly I could barely hear the people talking over the thumping in my ears.

I rolled onto my side and sat up slowly.

The bed creaked under my weight and I froze. Not breathing, but instead listening and waiting for someone to come.

No one did.

They'd left the door partially open and as I got to my feet and moved over to the door, the voices became more distinct.

It was Claire.

So, I was still at her house.

Thank God for that.

Had I fainted? Or fallen over, or something? I didn't remember.

But that was definitely Claire and she was talking to a whole group of men from the sounds of all the deep throaty voices I could hear.

"So, we'll wait for her to wake up, and then I'll explain what's going on here." Claire laughed awkwardly. "It's gonna shock the pants off her, though."

I grimaced. I was keeping my pants on. No matter what they put in the water out here, I was not becoming a version of Claire. Shacked up with three men, pregnant, and letting my career slip through my fingers.

I'd worked too hard to make it through college and get away from my trailer-park parents to let go of my job now.

It gave me purpose, happiness, not to mention the money to pay my rent and save for the house I'd one day buy myself.

A house of my own. My greatest dream.

One day.

I took a deep breath, and put my hand on the bedroom door. I had to go to work, so I needed to leave this room and face the music, so to speak. But the idea of walking out into that lounge area with all those men made my heart pound and my throat thicken with stress.

Time to pull myself together. I'd handled much worse. I grabbed the handle and opened the door. The room went suddenly, deathly quiet as I stuck out my head.

My breath caught in my throat and my ribs tightened around my chest. *Damn...*

"Oh my God."

There were four of them! When had that happened?

"Nevaeh!" Claire rushed to my side and grabbed my hand

with her good arm, resting her fingers on my ulnar artery and looking into my face. "Are you okay?"

"Yeah, what happened?"

"Ah, well, you fainted."

"I fainted? Seriously?" I'd never fainted. Not a single time. Not during college, or my thousands of hours in the E.R. and the horrific surgeries I'd witnessed. Why would I faint now? "My iron is probably down. I've been exhausted lately."

There had to be a good explanation for this.

I tried to focus on Claire, but most of my attention was on two of the men in the room. They were the ones I'd seen this morning. The next-door neighbors. And they were staring at me like a hungry man would look at a juicy steak.

Like they wanted to devour me.

Like they'd never seen a woman before.

And unfortunately, my love-starved body was experiencing the same thing. Arousal curled in my belly, creating heat in my loins. And over perfect strangers. How utterly insane was that?

"Nevaeh, I think you should stay here for the night. We have heaps of room, and I don't think you should be driving."

I raised an eyebrow at my boss. "You know I don't call in sick —ever. Three years running and never had a sick day."

Claire frowned. "You've been unconscious for over half an hour. That's not normal, hun. And if you have to go back to the hospital, I insist on giving you an escort. Grayson and Aaron can drive you."

She indicated to the two hot men across from us and a shiver of excitement coursed down my spine. They were both gorgeous. Sex on legs. And judging by my reaction, clearly lethal for a weak woman like me.

"No. I'll be fine."

Claire gave me the look, the one she reserved for errant patients.

"You have two choices. You can call in sick, stay here overnight and drive yourself home in the morning, or Grayson can drive you back now. You know me, Nevaeh... and I don't back down easily."

Dex laughed from the couch. "Easily? How 'bout never?"

I shivered. From what, I wasn't sure. I wasn't cold, and funnily enough, I wasn't scared. But the way those two men, Grayson and Aaron, were looking at me, was causing major issues with my internal thermostat.

"Ah... you're not giving me much choice, Claire."

She grinned at me and I relaxed even more. This was a woman I trusted, and if she said I should stay, then I'd stay.

I wasn't letting two strange men drive me an hour back to the hospital.

"I'll stay here if you have the room. A good night's sleep would probably do me the world of good." I'd been pushing hard lately. Fifty, sixty-hour weeks most of the time. "But only if it's no trouble."

"No. No, not at all. You can sleep down here in Jay's room if you want, or Taylor's room upstairs. We all sleep in Dexter's room when I'm home."

My mind flashed with images of how they'd sleep together. Coiled and sensual and naked. Pressed up against one another, having fallen where they may after a hot session of sex.

Or maybe they lay like puppies. On top of each other and in a pile.

A giggle escaped my lips at the idea and Claire cocked her head at me. "What's funny?"

"Ah... nothing, I'll ask you later."

My face heated with a blush, and I was mortified to think I was so obviously being inappropriate in front of all these people.

Grayson, the huge, hot one, was backing towards the front door, "Ah, Claire, Brad will be getting home from work soon. Do you mind if we come back after dinner?"

Although he was talking to Claire, his gaze kept darting toward me.

I smiled at him, though I wasn't sure why I wanted to reassure him that everything was okay.

Everything was not okay. I'd fainted, a first for me, and was being told I wasn't allowed to go to work or go home. My two safe places. Well, as safe as a place can be when you have a stalker that tracks your every move.

"I'm going to put on some dinner," Jay said and headed off to the kitchen.

Dex kissed Claire and moved to the front door. "I've gotta talk to Dad about a few pack matters but will be back with Taylor soon."

Grayson was still standing by the door with Aaron, and my heart lurched to see them leaving. They were so much better looking than Dex. How could Claire go for her guys, when the ones next door were so much hotter?

Grayson's skin was so clear and healthy I wanted to rub my own face against his. Dexter grabbed Grayson and they kind of fell through the doorway.

Claire turned away to seize her phone and my brain clicked into gear. "Hang on a minute. Did he just say pack?"

What sort of person referred his family as a pack? A pack of what?

"Oh, yeah. It's just a nickname. There's a high percentage of men in the town. Not many females have been born in the last few generations, which is why the guys live together in triads."

That sounded like something out of a dystopian movie. "That's a bit strange. How many is 'not many'?"

In most communities there was generally an even amount of males and females born, as long as there were no rules about how many children one family could have.

That tended to outweigh the odds.

"Ah... none, actually."

"What? How is that possible?"

I stared at her, watching her face for signs of deceit or misunderstanding.

Claire shrugged. "They don't know. Dexter's and Taylor's moms were some of the last-born females in this town. From then, only males have been born. Which is why I'm hoping I have a girl in here." Claire stopped to pat her still-flat stomach. "Because that would be a miracle."

I looked away, toward the front door, a chill coursing down my spine. "So, you're telling me that out there is an entire town filled with sex-starved men, who haven't seen a woman in, what... days, weeks? Months?"

My stomach tightened until I wanted to be sick. Was this why Claire had lured me out here? To be some triad's woman? "I think I should go home, Claire. You can't keep me here. Not with this many men... I..."

I couldn't breathe. My skin was on fire. "Claire! I... I..."

My breath was wheezing in and out, and my lungs hurt too much. My mind raced with escape plans. The front door. I ran for it. Tripped on the rug and fell straight into the wooden door. My shoulder screamed with pain. But I didn't stop. I couldn't.

I grabbed for the door handle with sweaty hands, "No... no... no!"

I could feel them coming up behind me. I screamed out as I pulled open the door and raced down the stairs toward my car. My keys were in my pocket. I grabbed them and pulled them out. My hands shook and my heart pounded in my chest like I was running away from a bear.

"Hey, are you okay?" a man to my left called out to me, and as I beeped open the door I was grateful to see that he was smaller than all the others. Just a little taller than me, thin, and he had a kind face.

He jogged over, his eyes going wide as he took in my trembling form. "I'm Brad. Are you okay? You're as white as a ghost."

"I need to go home. Now. I can't stay here. You don't understand..."

"I probably don't, but I'm sure I can help you. Okay?" He put his hand out and touched my arm, and I didn't stop him.

The feeling of his fingers on my skin soothed all my anxiety. Instantly. Like he'd switched off a tap. The blood drained away from my arms and legs and the sky began to spin.

The man gasped and gripped my arm harder as I began to fall. He swept me up into his arms, and after the day I'd had, following the year I'd endured, I let the darkness pull me under.

4

―――――――

BRAD

She was heaven and angels, and perfection, all in one beautifully scented package. I took a deep breath through my nose, the heat of arousal racing through my blood like a driver speeding on the last lap of a five-hundred-mile race. "Whoa."

If this woman wasn't our mate, I'd bite my own ass.

People came running from everywhere, it seemed, and although on one level I recognized all of them, I pulled my mate into my chest and backed away from everyone.

"What on earth is going on here?"

"Give her to me, Brad." Grayson came toward me with his arms outstretched.

I didn't want to hand her over. Indeed, my teeth descended, and my wolf rose to the surface to fight the Alpha for the woman in my arms.

"It's okay, Brad. I know how you're feeling. She's our mate. I won't harm her." Grayson said soothing things, and I focused on his words to calm the animal in me.

"Okay." Finally, I let him take her and she began to stir in his arms.

"Why did she faint like that? Is she unwell?"

"No, don't you remember what Dex said about Claire?"

The memory hit me all at once. "Oh, yeah, that's right. The mating thing."

We began to walk to our house and Claire called out, "Bring her back to our place. I told her she could sleep in Jay's room."

I frowned at her and shared a concerned look with Aaron, who had appeared at the same time as Grayson.

Claire crossed her arms over her chest. "Grayson. Bring my friend back to my house."

Grayson did, and we followed. My head was spinning. Aaron was grinning.

"How long have you known about this?" I asked him, angry accusation in my tone.

"Like... two hours. We got home from town, caught wind of her scent and found her in Claire's house. We would have told you sooner if we knew where you were."

I nodded, unable to deal with the emotions coursing through my blood.

My arms and legs tingled, as though ready for battle. To run, to shift. I wanted to get rid of all this excess energy but didn't want to leave our mate.

"What's her name?"

Aaron smiled. "Nevaeh."

It was pretty, but what did it mean? Then it hit me, my brain rearranging the letters and coming up with the answer. I laughed, loudly, the tension in my body dissipating.

"What's so funny?" Aaron asked me and I waved at him to indicate not to worry about it.

Obviously, no one else had figured it out, and I'd explain later.

Grayson was putting Nevaeh down on the couch and she was sitting as stiff as a board, uncomfortable and embarrassed by the look of her red cheeks.

"I fainted again, didn't I?"

Claire nodded. "Yes. Told you. You need to stay put. I'm going to call the hospital right now, and you're going to take a few days off."

Claire walked into the kitchen with her cell phone and began talking to someone.

I walked past my Alpha and Dexter and moved to sit on the couch near my mate. Not close enough to touch her as I ached to do, but near enough to drink in the beauty and the scent of our 'Heaven'.

"Are you okay?" I couldn't help but ask.

"Yeah... I met you just now outside. Thank you for helping me calm down. I was... not coping."

"You looked like you were having a panic attack. Do you suffer from anxiety?" I'd read a lot about depression and anxiety in the human population. It wasn't something we wolves suffered from, fortunately.

"Yes, I do. Though it's usually under better control than that. Why, do you?"

"Ah... not exactly. But I do empathize with the idea that your life is spinning out of control, and you don't know how to change it."

I'd felt like that for years, and it was only in the last month when the hope of a mate had come into our lives that I'd started to feel a little better.

A tear slipped down her face and she huffed out a laugh. I moved over to her and sat right next to her. I couldn't help myself and she didn't seem to be afraid of me the way she was of the larger men in the room.

I reached up to cup her face and wipe the tear from her cheek. "Don't cry, beautiful."

I wiped her tear with the pad of my thumb and little shocks of awareness passed over my skin. She shivered and pulled away a little, but didn't move to another seat.

"What is that? Why do I feel so strange when you guys touch me?"

"Because you're our mate. We're meant to be."

"What?" Nevaeh lowered her eyebrows, glared at me with a stormy expression, then got to her feet so she could glower down at me from a height. I hadn't expected such an intense response.

"What the hell is that supposed to mean?"

Claire came around the couch and stood beside Nevaeh. "What's happened? What's going on?"

"He just told me we're meant to be, and I'm his mate. Claire, what the hell is this bullshit? What are you guys smoking out here? And why the hell are these men so big? I've seen professional football players who were smaller."

Claire suddenly took charge of the room. "I need everyone but the Omegas out while I talk to Nevaeh."

"But Claire..." The men began to complain.

She waved her hands at them. "No! You don't understand how confusing this is for us. Go to Grayson's house. Have some dinner and a beer. We'll call you back soon."

The Alphas and the Betas left with their metaphorical tails between their legs and as soon as the front door shut, I laughed. I couldn't contain it a moment longer. Jay joined in, and Claire gave me a stern stare. "This is no laughing matter, Brad."

I grinned at her, the lightness and happiness in my heart making my head feel woozy. "I understand that, but you need to know that I have never, in all my life, seen anyone boss around the Alphas the way you do. It's awesome. Truly."

Jay chuckled from beside me. "It's true, Claire. And we love you for that."

Claire huffed at us, but her bright smile was returning. "Well, I'm not scared of them. Those muscles of theirs are for protection, not to cause us harm."

"So true." I nodded at her and gave her my best smile. "Still doesn't change the fact that watching you go up against them is awesome." I looked straight at Nevaeh. "Take note, seriously. Grayson and Aaron are big teddy bears, and you'll soon be bossing them around the way Claire does with Dexter and Taylor."

Nevaeh gave me a glare that was quite ugly, and it twisted my gut.

"Why are you looking at me like I've done something terrible?"

Nevaeh's face crumpled and although she didn't smile, the glare lost its strength. "You haven't. I'm sorry. I just don't know what I'm doing here."

Claire and Jay got up and moved around the kitchen, preparing food. Maybe.

I turned my attention back to my mate. "Tell me about yourself, Heaven spelled backwards."

Her face screwed up and she looked skyward. "I hate my name so much. Bloody hippie parents."

I couldn't stop myself from reaching out to her. But she slid away before I could feel her skin beneath my palm. That hurt. And it shouldn't have. The poor girl didn't know me, even though it felt like I'd known her my entire life.

I cleared my throat and pushed away the feeling of rejection that had no place in this situation. Not yet, anyway. "Why do you hate it so much? It's beautiful."

She rolled her eyes and groaned. "Because it has been the bane of my existence since high school. At home it wasn't too bad.

My mum called me her angel sent from heaven because she'd been told she couldn't have children, so to her, I was a miracle."

"That's really nice."

And it was. I'd feel the same way about any children I had.

"Yeah... I suppose, but it's given every guy, or bitchy girl who's not liked me, the perfect way to tease me."

"What would the guys say?"

She looked at the floor and began imitating a man's voice. "Oh, you sure look like heaven. Heaven on a stick, sex on a stick. You must have been sent from Heaven. You feel like Heaven. Blah, blah, blah. They made me feel so dirty all the time."

The words were just spilling out of her now. "Not that I'm complaining, but how come you're suddenly talking? You were practically rendered mute before."

Nevaeh's gaze met mine. "I don't know. I just... don't like being around too many people. Or big guys. This is nice. I feel less... threatened with just you."

She glanced back toward the kitchen, where Claire and Jay were working together.

So, she didn't like being intimidated or outnumbered. That was going to be a problem in our family. "I can understand that. You were an only child?"

She nodded, though her posture became guarded. "Yeah, why?"

"Because it makes more sense why you want to be around less people, so to speak. I grew up with three older brothers, so I feel lonely if there aren't at least three people in the room."

She rubbed her hands together, appearing to think about my observation.

"Three brothers? That would have been nice. I always wanted siblings."

"Maybe you still can, you know... have a big family when you're ready."

She shook her head. "No. I don't think so. I'd have to find a man I could trust enough to marry and have children with, and that's not going to happen any time soon."

That didn't sound normal, so I continued to ask questions. "How come?"

She cocked her head. "Why do you make me feel safe when the others make me want to run to my car and drive away?"

I laughed; I couldn't help it. "I always thought it was the curse of the Omega, but you're making me feel special, rather than inadequate."

"What are you talking about, Brad?"

I sighed as Jay and Claire sat down, placing platters of cold chicken and cut up vegetables before us. Perfect for chatting around the table while we ate. Jay was looking at me with understanding, and I realized now was the time to explain our world to my mate.

"I'll explain what I mean, but please be patient while I do, okay? It'll sound strange to you."

She grabbed a piece of chicken and nodded. "Okay."

"All right... well, in our town, there hasn't been a single female born in over fifty years, did you know that?"

"Yeah, Claire told me."

"Good. Well, the way the elders handled that had never been done before, but in retrospect, was kind of a brilliant move. They asked us guys, when we reached twenty-one, to make groups of triads. But we had to choose one Alpha, one Beta and one Omega for each family."

"And, other than ancient Greek letters, they are?" She smiled as if to soften her query, as she picked up a carrot and crunched on it.

"They're a..." I wasn't sure exactly how to explain it, especially to a human.

I looked to Claire for help and she smiled. "They're a classification, so to speak. For size, job and personality traits."

"Okay, so you're an Omega?" Nevaeh looked over at me, but Claire sat forward in her chair and took over the conversation.

"After you see it once or twice, you'll recognize it each time. An Alpha is the leader, and the largest of the three. He'll be the most possessive and physically huge, like Dex and Grayson. But they're teddy bears. Gray even more so, actually. A Beta is next. They're the Alpha's right-hand man. Slightly smaller but still fast and strong, and also extremely protective."

"And an Omega is the smallest and the nicest?" Nevaeh asked, shooting a tiny smile my way. "Is that why you thought being an Omega was a curse?"

I shrugged, but I liked her description. "Yeah, what can I say? I hated being the smallest of my family, both as a kid, and now. I can't run, hunt or lift the way Gray and Aaron do. I could train every day for the rest of my life, and I'll never be as naturally strong as Gray."

Nevaeh smiled more widely this time. "But if that makes you the nicest one, why would you care about all their puffy muscles?"

I laughed. "I wouldn't describe them as puffy muscles, beautiful. But I appreciate the sentiment."

Nevaeh looked away and I realized my error. "Oh, sorry. That just slipped out."

When she looked up, her gaze was harder. "Can I ask you a question?"

"Anything."

"What am I doing here, really? I mean... I came to visit Claire, but there's something else, isn't there? And you know. Can you tell me?"

The heat of her awareness and focus bore down on me.

I didn't really want to tell her, and risk having her be mad at me. I wanted to remain in this moment where she was looking at me, with a clear, open face, wanting my help.

But it wasn't meant to be. I had to tell her the truth. "I can. But you have to promise you won't... freak out."

Claire laughed, but there was an edge to the sound. "Oh, she's gonna freak out, Brad. If you can't handle that, you can leave, and I'll tell her."

I straightened and tried not to snarl at the doctor. "I'm not going anywhere."

"Then tell her." Claire flicked her hand and indicated to Nevaeh, who waited patiently for me to spill the beans.

"Okay." I slid over and took both of her hands in mine. Amazingly, she didn't move away, but instead waited for me to speak, with wide eyes. "Nevaeh, you're our mate. Grayson, Aaron and mine."

"Your... mate. What do you mean?"

God, her eyes were beautiful. Aqua, flecked with silver and a rainbow of sky blues.

"It means you're meant to be ours. Our... wife. Our partner— whatever you want to call it."

Nevaeh withdrew her hands and stared at me with a strange smile on her face. It didn't look like a happy smile.

"You seriously think I'm going to believe that you and I are meant to be together? You're really nice, and very hot... but I don't know you."

Pride blossomed throughout my body at her compliment. No one had ever said I was hot. Ever.

"But you will. And you'll learn to love me and Grayson and Aaron. Just like Claire has done with her pack."

That's when I lost her. Her eyebrows flew up and her jaw snapped together like the clapping of hands.

"You've got to be fucking kidding me, right?"

The sarcastic tone wasn't subtle.

"Ah... nope. Personally, I'd love to keep you all to myself, but you fainted at Grayson's touch, and Aaron's too, from what they said. So, you have to be everyone's mate in our triad. That's what the fainting thing means. It's how it works."

"I fainted... What? Hang on... What are you saying?"

Nevaeh abandoned her food and stood up to throw her hands around and yell.

"Because this better be a joke, Brad! Seriously. I am not getting sucked into your weird cult where there's some sort of upside-down polygamy thing going on. I don't even want one husband, let alone three! What the hell would I do with you all?"

Histrionics was how they used to describe it, and for the first time in my life I thought how blessed I was, not to have grown up with a sister.

"Nevaeh, calm down."

"Calm down? Calm down? You fucking calm down. I'm out of here, and if any of you— Claire, this goes for you too—tries to stop me leaving, I swear to God, you will be sorry."

She found her keys and, despite her threat, I ran to the door to block her exit. I had to convince her we were meant to be, and I had no idea how to do that.

"Nevaeh, can't you feel the connection between us? The attraction? You have to feel something. We do. And Claire said she knew straight away when she met her triad that they were meant for her."

Nevaeh stormed up to me. "Get out of my way, Brad. Now. Or I will call the cops and have you guys arrested! I already have one restraining order up on my ex. I'll happily put one on you, too."

I fell away from the door and Nevaeh yanked it open. While my heart was breaking, I heard a feminine chuckle from Claire behind me.

"Fight it all you want, Nevaeh. But you're never winning this battle. You're meant to be theirs, and you will be."

Nevaeh let out a feral growl as she stomped to her car, slammed shut the door, and drove away. A cloud of dust billowed up around the spot where her car had once been.

Claire and Jay walked up to me and Claire patted my arm as I stood there gaping at the empty space. "That actually went better than I expected." She laughed as she walked away, but my heart fell.

Had I driven our mate away for good? "What did I do wrong, Jay?"

Claire's Omega stood with me as I stared after the retreating car. "Nothing, Brad. You forget how weird this must be to a human, especially one who's been abused by a man like Nevaeh. Wait until you have to tell her you guys are wolf shifters. That one will likely go down like a lead balloon."

Jay walked off and the other men came running at me.

"What happened?" the Alphas demanded.

"I just..." I swallowed hard around the lump in my throat. "I told her about the three of us and she lost it. Screamed at me and drove away. I didn't even get to tell her about... anything, really."

Grayson grimaced. "Unfortunately, it sounds like Nevaeh's background will dictate her actions."

He sniffed the air and frowned. "Do you smell that?"

Aaron and I turned our heads in the direction Gray was looking, and there it was, faint, but definitely noticeable.

"Bears," I said.

"At least one. Dex!"

Dexter came to the door and Grayson called out, "There's a bear shifter around. We're going after our mate. You keep yours safe."

Grayson began to strip and we joined him in dropping our clothes.

"Okay, but be careful," Dex said. "The closer you get to town, the more dangerous it is for you with hunters around."

We nodded, before the shift ripped through the three of us at the same time.

My eyes transitioned to ones with great night vision, my hearing and sense of smell intensified, and the thrill of the hunt curled up my back as I dropped to my paws and shook my coat.

Grayson put back his head and howled to the sky. Then we took off after the woman meant to complete us.

5

NEVAEH

Can you bloody believe it? They expect me to... I couldn't even finish the thought! They expected me to.... I burst out laughing, in a strangely hysterical way.

How was it possible that today had gone so incredibly wrong? Claire... dating not one, but three men at once. And her next-door neighbors expecting me to do the same thing with them.

"Over my dead body!"

I was too hot in the car and rolled down the window to let in some fresh, night air. The strangest sounds met my ears. Deep growling. I tried to keep my eyes on the dark road ahead, but my gaze kept darting to the side to see if I could catch a glimpse of whatever was making that noise.

A bear?

Wolves, maybe?

I pushed myself to concentrate on the road before me. I didn't recognize any of the landmarks and the road was winding in a way that required my attention.

My heart began to thump harder in my chest. My stomach twisted until I tasted acid in my throat. This was bad. I shouldn't have left Claire's house. They weren't going to hurt me. I would have been safe.

Sure, Brad was saying crazy, stupid things about me being his mate... or something like that. But they wouldn't have hurt me. Claire wouldn't have let them.

And now I was driving in the dark, in bum-fuck nowhere, surrounded by weird animal growling noises. And I was scared. Despite the curves in the road, I pushed my foot down harder on the accelerator and turned on the radio to drown out the external noises.

Some stupid guy singing a dumb, stupid, love song came on the radio, and even though I'd usually switch it off with an angry flick of my wrist, I didn't care. I needed the distraction.

My heart thudded against my rib cage. Maybe I should turn back? I was still closer to Claire's house than home, and I could always head home in the morning.

I took my foot off the accelerator, slowing down in preparation to turn back. That's when I heard it. The roaring of an enraged beast.

And then a huge bear charged out of the darkness, straight at my car.

"No!" I screamed and jumped on the accelerator again. The car burst forward at the same time the bear plowed into the backseat door on the driver side, buckling the metal.

The car spun out of control and I braced myself for the impact. I kept screaming as I was flung around and around. My breathing came in spurts and pants, and I could hear the continued growling.

My car came to a rest, and thank the heavens, didn't roll. My neck was killing me and my shoulders were rigid as I gripped the steering wheel, but there was no blood. No broken bones.

An enormous black bear shuffled into view, visible in the headlights. Its terrifying gaze met mine through the windshield, and fear flashed through my body as I grappled for the keys. Would the car re-start?

I needed to get out of here. Now!

Then a wolf appeared. A big, silver wolf, and I think I must have passed out from sheer terror then, because I only remember flashes of what happened after that.

The vicious noises of an animal fight. The sinking feeling of knowing I was about to die. And realizing how stupid I'd been, to race off into the darkness in an unknown area of wilderness.

My pride had gotten the better of me again... No, not pride. My temper.

Someone was carrying me. I should have been scared. Who had me? Where were they taking me?

I half-emerged from the fog around my brain, but then the blackness took me again and the next time I woke up I was warm, in a bed, with a woman hovering over me.

"Claire..."

I quickly closed my eyes again. The pain in my head was like a hammer pounding on my skull.

"Take these," she said. "It'll help with the pain."

I put up my hand and took the pills Claire handed me. "Thanks."

She held a glass of water for me, and I washed the pills down my tight throat. I struggled to open my eyes, but eventually forced myself.

Claire was not the only one in the room. I let my gaze roam around. There were the three next door neighbors, all hovering like expectant parents.

And they were all shirtless. They wore jeans, but nothing else.

The most embarrassing part of it all was, despite my confusion and soreness, my attraction to them flared, flooding my belly and between my legs with the certainty that I desired them. All three of them. I winced at my traitorous body.

"Um... why are they not dressed?"

Claire crossed her arms over her chest. "If I tell you the truth, do you promise not to stomp off like a toddler and get into another car accident?"

I nodded quickly, dragging my eyelids up to focus on Claire's face. "Tell me."

Claire gave me one of her stern looks, one she usually kept for her wayward patients.

"Okay. I'm going to spill this out all at once, because I've been through it myself, and I can tell you, it's fucking... unbelievable. And amazing. And perfect. But I know you, and you're going to fight it with everything in you."

I wet my lips with my tongue, my focus returning as the pain receded into the back of my mind. What on earth was she about to say? "Tell me, Claire."

"This is a town full of wolf shifters. All the men, and the women, can change into a wolf at will. Yes, it sounds crazy, but it's true, and the guys can show you when you want them to... But it'll freak you out, I guarantee it."

If only Claire knew. I'd been introduced to the paranormal world already, several years ago now, when something horrific had happened. Something so bad, that I had managed to block it out of my mind. Until now.

So, hearing about shifters was surprising, but it didn't completely freak me out like it would if I hadn't had that earlier experience. "Wolves... I heard wolves in the woods tonight."

"Yes. Grayson, Aaron and Brad shifted, and followed your car when they smelled bear shifters in the area. They fought one of them, a large black bear, and Brad was injured."

I turned my head to look at Brad. Claire walked across and

turned him around. His back was slashed, blood still dripping down his beautiful skin.

I sat up straight, pain ripping through my head, but I fought back the wave of nausea. "Oh my God. Brad, I'm so sorry."

Brad turned back to face me, his eyes focused on mine. "You're worth any amount of pain."

I looked down and shuffled back so that I was resting against the bed head.

"Is that everything, Claire?" I swallowed hard as my voice shook, but I forced myself to keep going. "I mean not that... that isn't enough. But I feel like there could be more?"

Claire nodded, "There is. The truth is, these three are your mates. Fate, as it was, has chosen you to be with them. Love them. Marry them—however you want to put it. As Fate chose me for my three."

Shock ricocheted through me like machine gun fire, one bullet after another, puncturing everything I knew about myself. I'd believed I was meant to be alone. Apparently not.

I wasn't good enough for anyone to love. Or so my ex-boyfriend said. But what was Claire saying now, right in front of me?

"Let me get this right. You think that these three, men, if I can call them that..." They did, after all, allegedly turn into wolves if they wanted to, so I wasn't sure on the exact terminology. "Are my... husbands?"

"Well, mates is a better term for it. Grayson is your protector, Aaron would die for you, and Brad will be your best friend and companion forever. They are everything you've ever wanted in a man, and so much more. I'm telling you this to save you some time, but it probably won't help. You're even more stubborn than me."

I'd give her that, she was probably right. "Ah... okay. What do you want me to say, Claire?"

"I want you to say that you'll stay here for a few days. We need to identify the bear shifter who was following you, and I think you owe it to your triad, and yourself, to see if you can make this work."

I knew who the bear shifter was. Or at least, part of me did, even though I didn't want to believe it. One night, I'd seen a man turn into a bear, but I'd spent years convincing myself it was a nightmare. A bad memory that needed to be blocked.

And it had been. Mostly. "I... ah, can do that." What choice did I have?

Claire looked at me strangely once again. "You're taking this too well."

I took another sip of water. "Well, to be honest, I don't have much energy left to fight, and after what just happened, I doubt my car is drivable."

I glanced across to Grayson, meeting his gaze for the first time since I'd woken. He was a wolf shifter? And so intense. His eyes dug into my soul, deep, where I kept only the darkest of my desires and secrets.

My stomach fluttered and my heart squeezed. And I knew...

I knew.... They were right. There was something mythical and magical about this place. About these people. These shifters.

And I knew they were telling the truth about these men, and the fact that all three of them were my mates. But how was I ever going to let them into the walled-up fortress my heart had become?

And when they found out what sort of person I was... they'd never stick by me. No one would. I was one hundred percent sure of that.

6

GRAYSON

*L*ooking at my mate and staring deep into her eyes for the first time ever, made me want to drop to my knees and thank the heavens for their gift.

It also made me want to run. To shift. To rip apart the man responsible for her car accident. My fingers curled into fists and I tightened them, fighting the inner demon that threatened to overtake me.

"Thank you for saving me, for bringing me back to Claire tonight," Nevaeh said, staring first at me, and then at Aaron and Brad in turn.

I nodded once, feeling my teeth descend.

She stared at them, then jerked her gaze to Brad, who chuckled. "Grayson is having trouble controlling his wolf. I don't think he can talk."

Nevaeh pulled up her blankets in a move that indicated fear. I couldn't have that. I forced my wolf down and my anger back inside.

"It's... not you. I am... angry that the bear shifter got away." I took some breaths, calming the racing of my heart. "I'm sorry you were in that accident at all."

Claire began to back toward the door. "I'm going to go put the kettle on so I can make Nevaeh a hot cup of cocoa, then she's going to sleep. You three have five minutes before I kick you all out."

I smiled at the diminutive female. The very fact she could joke about such a thing lightened the mood in the whole room. She left us, though the door remained wide open, and we moved slowly toward the bed.

"Is there anything we can get you before we go?" I asked Nevaeh, stepping close and reaching out to touch her leg.

She pulled back, shrinking into the pillows.

"What's wrong?"

"I know you guys are probably, like, naturalists or something. But could you cover up a bit? You're intimidating me."

Brad grabbed one of Jay's shirts and pulled it on, then sat on the bed with her.

Aaron and I had to walk out to the lounge room to pull on the shirts we'd left on Claire's doorstep.

Claire was laughing from the kitchen.

"What's so funny, Doc?" I asked her.

"I knew she'd have an issue with you guys being half naked. I didn't want to say anything because everyone was so tense in there, but just so you know... humans aren't used to massive muscle-bound guys walking around, looking like that."

I glanced down at my now-covered body. "Okay. Thanks for the tip."

So, we would stay clothed. At least until she got used to us. We crept back into the room, where Brad was sitting next to her.

"You're okay with Brad more than us?"

Dex had explained that Claire had been the same, less intimidated by the Omega's size. Unfortunately, it hurt me to know I was her least preferred. Why didn't she see that I was here to love her, to protect her? I was the one who had driven that bear away.

"Well... he's not as big as you guys. My ex was really tall, and muscly, like you."

I shuddered against the jealousy that crawled up my skin. "And this ex-boyfriend... He hurt you?"

Her gaze dropped instantly and I knew we'd come to the root of the problem. I walked closer and dropped to my knees before her.

I was now looking up at her from the most submissive position I could manage. I wasn't sure if she knew how difficult this was for an Alpha, but I didn't care. I would do this, for Nevaeh. Her shoulders relaxed as the power of the situation was released and given to her.

She gave me a tentative smile.

"Nevaeh, I'd never hurt you. Quite the opposite. I'd die to protect you. So would Aaron, or Brad, for that matter. You need to know that, because anything less would shame us all."

Her gaze met mine and love wove through me, binding me to her. She gasped and put a hand to her chest. "What is that?"

I smiled. "The magic of the bonding. It will get stronger with time and you will learn to trust it. But please, we only have another minute or so."

"One minute exactly," Claire called loudly from the kitchen.

I rolled my eyes and Nevaeh's lips kicked up into a smile— this one more sure.

"Tell me what he did to you, so that we can go about repairing the damage."

"I'm not broken," Nevaeh declared, straightening her spine, her voice taking on a tone of indignation.

I laughed. "I know you're not. You're perfect. But I need to prove to you that I'm not like this last... man. So, I need to know what he did."

Claire walked in with a hot drink and placed the mug next to Nevaeh on the bed. She didn't try to make us leave, she only waited for Nevaeh's answer.

"He, um... Well, he hit me, for one thing."

Our gasps could be heard around the room, then Aaron's low, dangerous growl.

I put a hand out and touched Nevaeh's knee gently. "Please continue."

"Um... it's hard to explain. It seemed he didn't even like me, but forced himself to be with me. But it wasn't always that way. He was nice at the start, but that soon changed. Telling me how stupid I was. How, when he hit me, I made him to do it. He told me I was a curse to him, a poison to everyone around me. I broke up with him, but he would follow me. Send me threatening messages. I've tried to get away from him, even moved three times, left the city and came back here. But he... he's obsessed with me, or something."

She trailed off and I got the hint that she wasn't telling me everything.

"Is there anything else?"

She shook her head, her long, brown hair falling over her face. There was. She was hiding something, but only time would allow her to trust me enough to tell me. I was sure.

"Okay. Well, Claire's sending us back to our house for the night. But if you need us, we are literally one house away."

I stood up and she looked at me, her eyes wide and frightened as she took in my size.

I couldn't stand it. I bobbed down and rested on my haunches. "Give me your hands, beautiful girl."

She didn't, so I unbuttoned my shirt slowly. When she didn't move, I picked up her hands and put them against my skin. "I'm huge because I'm the Alpha of my pack. It comes with my genetics, it's not a choice. It's not for intimidation. It's not to hurt you. I'm strong so that when a bear comes for you, I can literally beat him to death, if need be."

She flattened her palms against my skin, "Did you kill him tonight?"

She sounded... strangely expectant.

"Ah, no. It was more important to get you back here. Why? Do you know who the bear shifter is?"

Nevaeh withdrew her hands, and the cold that flew in to replace her warm palms was like ice on my skin. "No. I just... You said..."

"I said I could protect you. That is the reason I am so big and strong."

I stood up again and walked to the door. She was lying to me. And I wanted to find out why. But perhaps tonight was too soon. "Claire, we're right next door if anything happens. You have our numbers."

"Yes. Thank you, Grayson."

Aaron and Brad came to the door also and bid our mate goodbye, and we all left, retreating to our home.

It hurt to do so. I can't deny it. But we were playing a long game in this moment, and I needed to remember that the only important thing at this time was Nevaeh feeling safe.

Thus, our mate would sleep beneath Dex's roof tonight, though it rankled me extraordinarily.

"What's going on with her?" Aaron asked, as we stomped inside our house and began to pull food from the fridge.

None of us had eaten properly and it was time to take stock of what was happening.

"What do you think she's hiding?" Aaron asked.

I grabbed some leftover pasta and began forking it into my

mouth. "I think she knows who the bear shifter is. And I bet you it's that douche bag of an ex-boyfriend of hers."

"Really? Well wouldn't that be an odd bit of luck?"

I shook my head, shoveling more food into my starving body. "It's not luck. There's something else going on here. I just need to figure it out."

"What do you mean?" Brad asked, eating himself through half a leftover pizza.

"It's too much of a coincidence. That the bears have always been our enemies... that they came for Claire when they found out she was a mate of ours. Now to know that our mate dated a man who was abusive, and now keeps constant tabs on her... it's too much to be coincidence."

"He's big like you, too, and the bear we ran into in the forest was aiming to take her car out specifically. He was a black— they're Alphas, I believe," Brad finished off for me.

Aaron groaned after he downed his beer. "So, we need to find out more about this ex of hers, and if all of this is some sort of crazy coincidence, or if the bears are finding our mates and keeping them from us."

"Oh my God. Imagine if that were true." I stared at my pack, my friends, my family.

The very idea that was possible completely floored me. There could be so many women out there under the same threat.

"This could be so much bigger than we know," Aaron said with a massive sigh.

I nodded, my gut tightening and gripping with fear for my mate. Sure, I'd felt anxious, tired, hurt, even depressed over the fact that I may never have a mate.

But now that we'd met her, and I knew she was next door— well, my wolf was pacing and circling inside of me like a restless animal.

"We sort out our mate first. We need to get Nevaeh to trust

us, love us. Then we can find out if this is part of a bigger plan to keep our mates away. The whole pack may need to know."

We went to bed early, and I tossed and turned all night. I needed my mate beside me. In my arms, in my house, in my life.

And tomorrow, I would find a way to have it all.

7

NEVAEH

Claire gave me a sleeping tablet, and I still had a bad night's sleep. I kept seeing that massive bear coming for me. And my guilty conscience weighed on me like a fridge laying across my chest.

I'd lied to them.

I did know who that bear was who attacked my car last night. Or, I think I did. It was Trevor, my ex. Or one of his biker friends. They all turned into bears, or so Trevor said. Deadly, vicious bears. And he'd said that if I told anyone, he'd kill me. One of his many, many threats.

I'd tried to block out so much of that part of my life. Away. Hidden in the depths of my subconscious. But here it all was. Spilling out for the world to see.

"Good morning," Claire said as she opened the door to my bedroom—Jay's bedroom.

"Oh, hey." I sat up, wearing some of Claire's spare joggers and a tank.

They were too big for me, and perfect for sleeping in. "How'd you sleep?" she asked, and I shrugged.

She laughed knowingly. "You slept like shit because your mates are next door and you aren't with them. I know the feeling."

I looked at her, my head spinning with all the information they were all throwing at me.

"You know how surreal this feels, Claire? Yesterday I was single, happy, and focused on my career. And today you expect me to believe I'm 'meant to be' with three complete strangers? Men who aren't whom I'd choose for my husband anyway."

Claire gave me the eye. "You mean because they're hot, horny and too dominant?"

I looked away.

"Don't ignore me, Nevaeh. I know you want a guy you can control, who's totally harmless. Short, chubby and less intelligent than you."

Tears sprang to my eyes as she vocalized the exact thoughts I'd had. I wanted someone who wouldn't hurt me. And a chubby computer programmer sounded about right.

"Look at me, Nevaeh."

I dragged my gaze back to Claire, now sitting on the edge of the bed.

"But that isn't what you need, and you know it."

"Oh, really? You're gonna tell me what I need?"

Even as I said it, I knew Claire had an answer for me.

"Of course, I will. You need a guy who's strong and passionate and smart and amazing. Just like you are. The best part of having a triad is that you're never lonely, and if one of them doesn't have what you need in any given moment, one of the others will."

"What do you mean?"

Claire grinned. "Well, for example, Dex hates cooking and so do I. So, Jay and Taylor do most of that. Jay's super-affectionate and smart, and Taylor can build anything you could think of. No matter what I need, one of them will always fit the bill."

I hadn't thought of it like that. "Look, Claire, it sounds great in theory, but I couldn't imagine letting a guy like Grayson, who looks just like Trevor, anywhere near me. I know you said he's a sweetheart but..."

Claire groaned and stood up. "Look, hun. Give them a chance, okay? This Trevor guy sounds like a narcissistic asshole, and Grayson may be many things, but he is not that."

"How do you know?"

"Well, for one thing, the bear shifters attacked a month ago. They came for me."

Shock rolled through me. They came for Claire? Why?

"What happened?"

She shrugged. "They didn't even get into the house. My mates and yours stopped them. Grayson, Aaron and Brad all risked their lives for me that day, and they've been perfect gentlemen ever since."

I couldn't even imagine men being that selfless. "I don't know what to say."

"Say you'll give them a chance to prove to you that they are who they say they are. Because I will vouch for them, Nevaeh. I will. They're hard-working, extremely sweet and you have to admit... pretty bloody hot."

A smile kinked up my lips, though I tried not to let Claire see it. "Yeah... they are good looking. But that's part of the problem— my attraction for hot guys in the past has gotten me in trouble."

Claire literally threw her hands up in the air, or her non-broken arm, anyway.

"Fine! You know what? Go! Go back to your old, lonely life, and I'll see you at work."

Claire stomped off toward the door and I jumped to my feet.

"Wait! Claire, that's not fair. You don't know what it's like to have a guy hurt you the way Trevor hurt me."

Claire turned back to stare at me. "Yeah, maybe I don't. But you know what I know? That asshole men are always bad lovers, even when they're being nice and trying to suck you in. Do you agree?"

I shuddered and nodded. Sex had always been terrible with Trevor. I'd tried to believe that his speed in coming and lack of caring was because he wanted me so much.

But the lack of intimacy, touching and caring afterwards never made sense.

"Yeah, I agree. Men are always selfish lovers, though. All the girls at work say it. Even the good husbands are bad in bed."

It was a biological problem. The continuation of the species was not contingent on whether we had an orgasm or not. It was all about them.

Claire gave me a smug smile and crossed her arms over her large breasts.

"Well, I can tell you that they're wrong. My men are amazing in bed. Give me non-stop attention and don't come until I'm fully satisfied."

I just stared at her. That wasn't possible.

"And I guarantee that if you go to bed with your triad, you'll find out the same."

Heat surged up my face, and into the lower half of my body. "Why would I do that?"

"Because you want to know if they're different than your ex? That's the perfect test. No man can hide his selfishness in bed. It all comes out when the pleasure is there for the taking."

"But I... wouldn't even know how to... Even if I wanted to..."

Which I didn't. My body screamed out in pain at my lie. I wanted to. God, how I wanted to. It had been years for me. I was practically re-virginized, or so Google said.

Claire chuckled. "Go over to the house and see them. Let your guard down, and I guarantee you'll end up in bed with them. The mating attraction is too strong for them to resist, and in the end, you'll fall for it, too."

I indicated my clothes. "I don't have anything to wear. Wait I think I packed a change of clothes for after night shift."

I hadn't even thought about it until now.

"Good. Have a shower and some breakfast, get changed, and go spend some time with your triad. If you're not convinced that they're different from any other man you've ever known by the end of the day, I'll drive you back to Little River myself. Tonight."

She left the room and began puttering around the kitchen. I sat back down on the bed, more confused than ever. If I were completely honest with myself, I was very attracted to the three men who saved me last night. Grayson, most of all. Which I hated myself for. Why did I have to want the guy with the biggest muscles?

I sighed and got to my feet once again and walked through the lounge room toward the front door. "Oh, shit... my car. My clothes... How do I get to them?"

"Eat this, and Grayson will probably take you to your car, if you want." Claire shoved a plate of toast and fruit at me.

"Okay." What else could I do?

I shuddered at the idea of going back to the scene of the accident.

"Actually, it might be better for me just to stay here. Do they have any shops for women's clothes?"

"They do, but they're pretty plain. Jeans, sweaters. Not much call for them, at least for younger women, here."

"Works for me."

I was most at home in a tank and jeans anyway. No bra if I could help it. My breasts were small enough to get away with that most of the time. I ate the food in front of me and finished the glass of water Claire gave me.

There was a single knock on the door, then the front door opened, and Grayson walked in. His huge presence and smile made me jump to my feet, my heart pounding against my ribs.

What was it about him that I was so attracted to? I couldn't put it down to just one thing. He was gorgeous, sure. The symmetry of his features, the strength of his jaw and the fact that his body could grace the cover of any sports magazine in the country certainly helped.

But I'd never felt anything like this before. Not for any man, and definitely not for Trevor.

Grayson made me want to walk over to him and kneel in front of him. My mind went far further than my conscious thoughts dared and it made my cheeks flame with heat. What was this?!

Surely it had something to do with the fact that he had saved my life yesterday? Or the fact that I hadn't had sex in years, literally.

But after Claire's suggestion of testing out the men on their giving natures in bed, I couldn't get the thought out of my head. Because, despite my initial horror at her suggestion, it now made perfect sense. I just had to work out a way to "seduce" them into it. Though, from the heated look I was getting from Grayson, it may not be a problem.

"Good morning, Nevaeh."

"Good morning," I said, pulling the tank down at the front, conscious of how fat this top made me look.

I was naturally quite thin, though Trevor had always pointed out how big my ass was in comparison to my boobs. Not that I had a choice about that one. Plastic surgery wasn't in my scope, not this early in my life.

"Nevaeh needs to buy some clothes that fit her. Would you

guys mind taking her to Sharon's shop?" Claire asked, with the casual calm of someone who was always in charge.

"Of course." Grayson said, quietly. Strongly. Without taking his eyes off me.

My lower belly tightened and clenched.

"Now?" I asked, my voice hopping in my throat. I needed a shower, but there was no point until I had clean clothes to put on.

"Sure. Aaron and Brad need to head off to work for the morning, but they'll be back for lunch."

I dragged my eyes across to the other two men, who both looked at me with the same hunger as Grayson.

But for some reason, the need to be close to the biggest man of the group was tugging at me.

"Great. I'll come now and walk with you guys, if you like?"

Their eyebrows flew up in identical signs of surprise. I almost laughed. Had I been that bitchy toward them yesterday? Probably. I'd been told more times than I could count that I was an ice queen, and a frosty bitch.

I grabbed the shoes I'd worn yesterday and pulled them on. I didn't know where my other clothes were. Knowing Claire, they were being washed or burned. I rushed to the front door and stepped outside into the bracing cold.

I inhaled sharply, wrapping my arms around my body as my skin prickled into goose bumps. Then, I was being surrounded by warmth and the smell of a man. A far too sexy man. A scent that was designed to drive me insane.

I looked up at Grayson, who'd taken off his jacket and wrapped it around me. "Thank you."

It was like being a kid wrapped in your parents' clothes. Too big, but so comforting.

He shrugged. "I thought you may need it."

I looked over to see that neither Brad nor Aaron wore jackets. Only tank tops.

He brought the jacket just to give it to me if I needed it? How thoughtful. "You guys don't get cold?"

Aaron shook his head. "Not really. If it's snowing, we need our jackets, but our wolf genes keep our metabolism burning pretty fast."

"Oh, I wish."

Brad looked at me strangely. "But you're very skinny. Why would you want to be more so?"

I wasn't sure how to even approach that. "Um... because I don't eat much. I'm sure you guys eat whatever you want and can stay as you are."

Brad took my hand and lifted it to his lips, kissing my fingers in a strangely intimate way. "I hope you learn to be happy here. In your own skin. Because you have to know that we will adore you no matter what you look like. It's one of the conditions of us being your mate."

I pulled my hand back gently. "What do you mean?"

We began walking along the road and I started to notice all of the other men. There wasn't a single woman my age, though I saw a few older ones.

I stepped closer to Grayson, who squeezed my waist once then let go, though he stayed close. "Don't worry, beautiful. None of them will come anywhere near you."

And somehow, I believed him. "Tell me more about this mating thing."

"Well, for one thing, none of the other pack members will want you the way we do. Dex was extremely possessive over Claire when they first met, but she just doesn't do it for us. She's nice, of course. But we aren't attracted to her."

"Don't like big boobs?" I joked and the men looked confused.

"Oh, it's not a literal attraction thing. We wouldn't care if you were even skinnier, or if you were twice as big as Claire. The attraction is a chemical one we can't control. You're our mate, and we'll never want another woman again. You're it for us."

I stopped in the street, and they all turned to look at me. "Are you kidding me?"

They couldn't possibly be telling the truth. Three men this hot couldn't be telling me that they would be faithful to me for the rest of their lives. It was impossible.

"No. What's wrong?" Grayson asked.

"We better go, Gray. You got this?" Brad asked and Grayson nodded.

Brad stepped forward and pressed a kiss to my forehead.

Aaron stood still, shaking in a strange way. Like he couldn't decide what to do.

"Bye," I said, waving at him and giving him as much of a smile as I could manage.

"Ah..." Aaron leaned forward, then turned and walked away.

When they were out of earshot, I asked Grayson, "What's wrong with Aaron?"

"He... um... It's hard to explain. Brad's bonded with you already, and I get my chance this morning. I think Aaron's jealous, or something. He hasn't really explained."

That made sense. How would three men share me anyway? "I kind of get it."

"Yes, I do too. But hopefully we'll have a lot of time together, so there's no need to hurry."

My body disagreed with him. The further I walked, the longer I spent with Grayson, the more my body ached.

Quite literally. My pussy throbbed and my nipples tingled. "Um... you were going to tell me more about the mate thing. You weren't serious about being faithful to me, were you? Not all of you."

It was impossible. Totally impossible. Male animals were seed spreaders. Not settle-down-and-commit types.

Grayson grinned. "Of course, we were serious. That's part of mateship. We won't desire another woman for as long as we live. None of us. We've found you now and we know what it feels like to have you close by. Anything else would be wrong."

"So, if I decide to return to town and stay single?" Which was the most likely thing at this point.

"Then we'll wait for you to come back."

He said it like there was no other choice.

"But what if I didn't want to be with you? If I wanted to stay single for the rest of my life?"

Grayson shrugged and opened the door to a shop. "Then we would wait. And if you decided you never wanted us, then we'd stay single, too. However, you have to understand that we're not going to go down without a fight."

His smile made my stomach quiver.

"What do you mean?"

He leaned forward and whispered in my ear, his hot breath causing a shiver to course down my spine. "I mean... I'd use all my seduction techniques to convince you otherwise. But after that, if you decide not to have us... Then again, I would wait."

When he stepped back, my knees trembled and buckled and I fell forward. Grayson caught me against his hard body and held me tight. I moaned and his hands slid lower, gripping my ass. My pussy tightened.

I had to get away from him. I couldn't think straight. "Ah, well... I'm glad you aren't one to give up easily or quickly."

I managed to get up again and walk into the store, though I could feel how hot my face was.

An older woman was standing behind the counter, her shock at seeing me a palpable thing. "Hello. I'm Sharon."

I walked forward and stuck out my hand. "I'm Nevaeh. I know I look ridiculous, but I had to borrow some of Claire's clothes."

She looked me up and down. "Size four?"

"I prefer a six," I said from pure habit.

She tsked at me, as older women were wont to do. "Why? Because you still feel like you're not skinny enough?"

She pulled clothes from her racks. Jumpers, jeans, tank tops.

"Well... um..."

She walked up to me and gave me a straight look in the eye. "You're perfect, and compared to all the women in this town, a good fifty pounds too light, so go try on some clothes that fit you."

I stared at her for a minute, then looked back at Grayson. "Um..."

"Do what she says. Everyone else does."

I took the jeans and moved into the change room. I wasn't sure what world I'd fallen into, but for the first time in a very long time, I felt truly safe.

8

———

GRAYSON

I smiled at my mom and watched her frown right back. "You didn't tell me, Grayson."

I fought to stop myself from bowing my head in shame. "We only found out yesterday. She was at Claire's house."

"We? You mean she's your pack's mate? Like with Dexter's pack?"

My mother sounded surprised.

"What's wrong, Mom?"

She crossed her arms over her rather large chest. "Oh, nothing. I just... Some of elders thought this may be a pattern, one mate per triad. I wasn't sure. But now..."

The curtain to the dressing room moved aside and a woman stepped out. One with long, flowing brown hair, thin legs and perky breasts that lifted her tank top.

Whoa.

"Everything's too tight," Nevaeh said as she tugged at her tank and the jeans that hugged her ass.

"No," my mother said, her tone one of someone who is not to be trifled with. "They fit your thin, perfect body. Not strong yet,

82

but you will be if you stay here with us. Now, go home, stay warm. There's a storm coming, and everyone needs to get indoors."

Mom packed the few extra clothes in a bag and handed it to me. "Take these. And, Nevaeh, put this on. The temperature's dropping."

My mom handed Nevaeh a thick wool sweater.

"How do I pay for all of this, Sharon?"

My mom stepped over to where Nevaeh was staring up at her like she was some mythical creature to behold.

Mom cupped Nevaeh's face and spoke softly. "You look after yourself and my son. Now, go on."

"Your son?" Nevaeh looked at my mom, probably assessing her face and seeing the same blue eyes that ran in all of my mother's sons.

She looked over at me with the softest expression. "This is your mom?"

"Yeah." I sighed heavily as Mom shoved us toward the door and flung the "open" side over to "closed".

"I wasn't joking about those storms, Gray. Get going."

I nodded and pulled Nevaeh into the street. My mother was never wrong about these sorts of things. The wind had turned, the air now biting into my skin with the sting of coming snow.

"Let's hurry."

We jogged across the street and in the direction of our house. I held Nevaeh's hand. The smallest, warmest hand I'd ever been able to touch.

"Almost there," I yelled over the wind.

People were running everywhere. I pulled Nevaeh closer as we pushed toward my house. She cried out as she stumbled, tripping over something on the ground.

I swept her up into my arms and walked on. When we got

home, I ripped open the door and had to walk in and push my back against the heavy wooden panel to get it to close.

When I set Nevaeh down, she was shivering. "Oh my God. How did that happen?"

"I don't know."

We didn't have heating in the house. All the homes in the pack were very well-made, and well-insulated, but without women, we hadn't bothered to put in fireplaces, or central heating. "We're going to have to keep you warm."

I looked around the room. We didn't have blankets hanging over the couches. Everything was either in a linen closet or in our bedrooms.

"Your house is beautiful. Different than Claire's."

Nevaeh didn't seem to be as worried as I was about the heating issue. She was staring at the walls, the kitchen, the intricately curved cornices with a look of fascination on her face.

"Ah, yeah. Brad's a plasterer and Aaron's a carver, so our house has details that some of the others don't."

"Cool," Nevaeh said as she wrapped her arms around her body and walked around the room, studying it in more detail.

I needed to get her wrapped in a blanket, and there were a few ways of doing that. "Would you like a tour?"

She nodded and I pointed to the study.

"Down here is pretty much like Claire's house. Kitchen, living space, laundry and a spare room we have set up through there. Upstairs are our three bedrooms and another lounge room and library."

"Library?" she asked, her eyebrows rising high as she took a few steps up the staircase.

"Yes, we all like to read. Learn. Especially Aaron. He's kind of the brains of this triad."

She nodded and walked up to the top of the stairs.

"Is this your bedroom?" she asked as she walked into my room. A place no woman had ever been.

"How'd you know?"

She smiled. "It's at the front of the house, so I suppose any offender would have to get through you, wouldn't they?"

"Yes." I prowled forward, watching as she took off her sweater and placed it on the bed.

She was looking around my room, seemingly innocent, but I could sense that something had changed in her chemistry. Her scent had morphed into something sweeter, hotter, somehow.

It appeared the choice now for me was to push forward or wait for Aaron and Brad to join us.

She sat on the bed. "It's so warm in here."

I walked forward and knelt before her, put my hands on her thighs and opened them, sliding between them with my body so I could look into her eyes. "Will you stay with us, just until we know if you feel what we do? That you're our mate and we're meant to be together."

In her eyes I saw so much vulnerability and fear, yet she didn't run. She cupped my face in her small, warm hands, and nodded. That was all the sign I needed. I leaned forward and kissed her.

She moaned as our lips met, and pleasure shook me to my very core. I slid my hands around her skull, through her thick hair and held her face to mine, sipping from her lips, tasting the inside of her mouth.

I kissed her until we were both breathless and the air around us was filled with the sounds of our sighs. I stood up and threw back the blankets, then pulled her to her feet.

"You look amazingly hot in those jeans, but I'm afraid I'm going to have to get you to take them off."

I reached for her jeans and she helped me undo them, pushing them over her lean hips and to the floor.

Next was her tank. Nevaeh lifted her hands so that I could pull the top over her head and then suddenly she was before me, standing in only her underwear.

Heaven.

"God, you're beautiful."

I kissed her again, wrapping my arms around her small body and loving the moans she expressed in her throat as we continued to kiss.

"Lie back."

She slid onto the bed and lay on her back, quivering.

"Are you cold?" I asked her, reaching for the blanket.

She shook her head emphatically. "No."

Her ribs were rising and falling at a rapid rate and I caught the scent of fear in the air.

"Don't be scared. I promise, I will never hurt you."

I slid onto the bed and moved over the top of her.

She reached up and encircled my neck, pulling me down.

I kissed her nose, her cheek, her forehead. Every inch of her had me dying to pleasure her.

Would she welcome me into her body at this point? I was pretty sure I could seduce her into just about anything.

But something told me to stop. A strong instinct told me to wait until my fellow pack mates were home to fully satisfy her.

That didn't mean I couldn't have a little taste to whet both of our appetites.

I slid down the bed.

She arched her back for me, and I moved my hand around to unclip her bra. With one flick of my hand, I discarded it.

She laughed. "That takes a lot of practice."

I shook my head as I moved down her body, kissing her breasts, suckling on the sensitive nipples that might one day feed my young.

"Practice for you, my mate."

She moaned loudly as I drew her nipple deep into my mouth. She dug her nails into my head and I moved lower. Until I finally found Heaven.

I knelt up on the bed and pulled her underwear down her long, thin legs. "Open up for me, beautiful."

She was holding her legs together, but on my command, she spread her thighs wide and showed me her pussy. She was so clean. So beautiful. So perfect.

"Is it okay... I mean I know it's ugly anyway, but I try to keep it as tidy as possible."

I looked away from her center, to her beautiful face. "Ugly? A man would kill to have this pussy in his bed. Who told you it was ugly?"

"Ah..."

Suddenly I wished I hadn't asked that question.

"Nevaeh. This is the prettiest..." I leant and kissed her clit and she gasped. "Most beautiful..." I ran my tongue down her center. "Most perfect pussy I have ever seen."

And as she was coming down from her third moan, I put both hands under her hips, grabbed her perfectly tight ass and got down to eating her properly.

She screamed as I set my mouth to her already swollen clit and thrust my tongue from side to side. Her moans vibrated in my ear as I worked my way down her slit, tasting her juices, then back up again, spreading her moisture and moaning myself as my cock swelled inside my jeans.

Keeping my clothes on had been the right thing to do. If I hadn't, this would be the perfect time to slide up her body, kiss her lips, and thrust my cock into her.

"Fuck! Grayson."

I groaned. Yep, that would have been the moment.

But that was for another day.

I moved one of my hands back out and slid my middle finger into her tight core.

She screamed again and arched her back, her pussy clenching onto my finger with a death grip.

Damn she's tight.

We'd have to be careful here.

I thrust my finger up and curled my digit, reaching for those hidden spots that would give her the most pleasure.

She began to pant and tighten and cry out.

I licked around her clit in large circles, then closed my lips around the swollen nub and moaned as her taste changed.

Her gasps grew louder, and she grabbed for my head, tugging at my hair.

She keened and arched as her body began to ripple around me.

I groaned as she screamed, her pelvis bucking beneath my mouth as she tried to both get closer and crawl away at the same time.

I withdrew my finger and slid up the bed, holding her in my arms while she shivered and shook. Her eyes rolled forward and back, her body gloriously naked.

Her nipples were tight and peaking.

That's when I heard the front door open and close.

My instincts told me to pull up the blanket and cover Nevaeh's perfect body.

But that wouldn't be fair to her, nor them. Because I was pretty sure my pack mates were going to want to pleasure our mate just like me.

Suddenly my door opened, and Brad and Aaron stood in the doorway.

"Come in, you guys have perfect timing," I said. "We were just getting started."

9

NEVAEH

The spasms in my belly spread through my whole body like ripples in a pond. I couldn't control them. The shudders and shakes rolled through me, and it was truly the most magnificent moment of my life.

I never knew it could feel like this.

Heat seared my eyes and slid down my face, completing this moment as a true first for me. Love and sex and orgasms. Just like all the romance novels said were possible.

Amazing.

"I... Um..." I swallowed, trying to get my bearings. Return to a sense of normality, whatever that may be.

No one had ever given me an orgasm before. Ever. Especially like that. I hadn't thought it was possible.

"We have company, beautiful girl. Are you ready for all of your mates to adore you?"

My stomach tightened and my eyelids popped open.

I lifted my head and forced my unfocused eyes to see the other two men standing in the room.

"Aaron... Brad..."

My insecurities once again swam to the surface of my mind and I could just imagine all the horrible things they were thinking after seeing my flawed body.

I reached for the blanket to cover myself.

Aaron and Brad stepped back, away from me, which wasn't what I wanted.

"If you want us to go, Nevaeh, we can go. We didn't mean to interrupt." Aaron's tone was hurt and I sat up, forcing myself out of my incredible bliss and looking at the men before me.

Surely, they weren't the ones feeling rejected, were they?

"I don't want you to go. I just... feel strange, being the only naked one in the room."

Brad laughed. "Oh, we can change that."

He dropped his jeans and stripped himself of his tank in mere seconds. Then suddenly, he was naked.

Gloriously, beautifully naked.

Brad's cock was already hard, pointing toward me, red and swollen.

I swallowed and dragged my eyes away from Brad's hypnotic shaft to Aaron, who still hadn't moved.

"You don't want to?" I asked him, a heavy weight pushing against my heart.

I didn't know how to take this man. He was darker, more intellectual in his approach, and from what I could tell, more hesitant than the other two.

Grayson had moved from his place beside me, and I kept my gaze averted. I wasn't sure I could look his way if he was naked, too.

All that strength....

I shivered and focused on Aaron.

He cleared his throat with a strangled cough. "Of course, I do, Nevaeh. You're my mate too, but I don't want to force you, or the situation. If you'd rather not..."

He glanced down and stuck his hands in his pockets, looking like an insecure adolescent in the principal's office.

It filled me with an empathy for his struggle, a need to reassure him.

"Aaron, would you..." I swallowed. I'd never asked a man this question before. "Would you make love to me?"

Would it be love for them? Is that how this mating thing worked?

I was certainly going to find out.

Aaron's head came up and his gaze caught with mine. His intense, dark eyes burned into me. I held his gaze, my body trembling with the hunger Grayson had woken in me.

Aaron didn't speak but he began to undress. His tank came off first and my breath caught in my throat. He was huge, like a wrestler. His waist was so lean it made his shoulders look even bigger. Every inch of his body was covered in rock-hard muscles.

He hesitated as he began to unbutton his jeans. "I'm bigger than Brad..."

It sounded like a warning. I was pretty sure he would be. In every way.

I nodded. "Show me."

The smile that kicked up Aaron's generous lips made my heart melt and tears linger once again in my eyes.

Was this what it felt like to fall in love? With kind, generous souls? His black jeans fell away to reveal huge thighs and a cock that bobbed up and down as though bowing in introduction.

I threw back the blanket that covered me and jumped off the bed to stand in the warm room. My throat thickened with embarrassment, but I pushed the feeling away. Instead, I walked the few feet separating Aaron and me and looked up into his face.

His beautiful, intense, strong face. He didn't reach for me, though I could sense that he wanted to. The control he was exerting over his own desire inflamed mine.

And the best part of it all was that by handing over the power to me, Aaron made me feel truly powerful. As though I could either stop this or go on if I wanted to. That was a heady aphrodisiac.

He wasn't moving, so it was my turn to go out on a limb. "Kiss me."

Then Aaron reached for me, one hand going around my waist and pulling me flush against his body, the other sliding into my hair.

I groaned at the first moment of skin-on-skin contact, heat and desire weaving through my blood.

My knees gave way. Aaron grabbed me against him and held me firm.

I lifted my thighs and wrapped my legs around his waist, holding on to his strong body. The move came naturally to me, as easy as breathing.

Aaron's groan filled the room before he whispered a word I'd always hated. "Heaven."

On his lips, pulled from his very soul, this moment we were sharing was exactly that, however. Heaven.

I wrapped my arms around his neck and pulled him into me for a kiss. Our lips met and sparks tingled on my skin. His tongue slid through my parted lips and he tasted me. I parried back, letting my eyes slide shut, and put all my pent-up passion into the kiss.

He moved us around the room and I held on until he was sitting down.

I opened my eyes to see that he'd brought us across to the bed. He was lying on the mattress and I was now straddling him, his cock lying on his belly in front of me.

Thick and hard, and so temptingly beautiful.

Aaron was breathing hard, but not moving us to the next

level. As I stared at him, I realized I needed to push all my doubts away and follow my instincts.

And my instincts told me to ride him.

I arranged my legs around him so I could lift up, and Aaron grabbed his shaft, holding himself upright for me.

I leaned forward, my already aroused and juicy body sliding over the massive head and welcoming him in.

I slid down a few inches, gasping with the intensity of it all.

"Fuck. You're so tight," Aaron groaned, reaching for my hands and shaking with the strain of staying still beneath me.

I raised my hands and linked our fingers, connecting on a level I'd never experienced with anyone.

My soul tugged at me, connecting and weaving together with Aaron's. But there was so much more to be had, I could feel it. I rocked my pelvis, swallowing as much of him as I could, over and over again, moving up and down.

"It's been... a very long time," I managed to say.

I was tight, and tender. But the soft pain made way for pleasure, and I needed more.

Aaron groaned again, louder this time, his fingers pressing into my hands. I pushed all the way down until I was sitting on his hips, his huge cock filling me right up.

My eyes flew open and I found Aaron's gaze on me. Not lost in the moment, not trying to take his pleasure from my body and depriving me of mine. He was focused, waiting. Sharing this with me.

"Tell me when you're ready to take me properly, beautiful."

I exhaled deeply, my belly finally relaxing around the intrusion.

I nodded. "Okay. I'm ready."

He moved his hands to my hips and I unlinked his fingers so that I could hold onto his arms.

"Let me know if you need me to stop, but I need you so damn much. This is going to be difficult to control."

I nodded, though fear shivered through me.

What was the worst thing that could happen? A bit of pain? I'd had a lot of that before.

Aaron grinned and planted his feet on the bed, then he began to move, thrusting up into me and moving me up and down on his cock in time with his own rhythm.

I gasped as pleasure shot through me.

I leaned forward to make the position more comfortable and even more pleasure raced through me.

I rode the wave with him, thrusting down as he thrust up, his moans and mine filling the room.

"Damn... you are so fucking perfect!" Aaron panted, and my pussy began to tighten. To ripple. The pleasure of my first orgasm made it so much easier to recognize the signs in my body, and reach out for my next one.

I held myself up and still as Aaron pumped into me, over and over again.

I threw back my head and let the waves of pleasure come. I screamed out as his cock pushed me over the edge, and his own orgasm was triggered.

Heat shot through me and caused an even greater orgasm to take over my body.

I shuddered and shook, falling forward to hear Aaron's groan as he filled me with his seed.

The pulse of heat like I'd never experienced made me moan with wonder.

It was perfect.

Aaron put his arms around me and rolled us, so I was on my back and he was softly kissing my lips, my face, and my neck.

I couldn't open my eyes at first, but as Aaron withdrew and

the weight of another person tipped the mattress, my need renewed. An ache in my core woke me out of my daze.

I lifted my eyelids to see my sweet Brad, sliding over me and on top of me with a smile.

"You ready for more, beautiful?" he asked, as he settled between my thighs.

He couldn't possibly be ready for me already?

"Don't you need—" I gasped as he lined up and thrust inside me. I groaned and lifted my legs to accommodate him. "Obviously not."

He kissed me, his lips sipping on mine. Feeding me while taking what he needed.

His pace was gentler and slower than Aaron's to start with, as he rolled his hips and took his time.

But need was clawing at me, making me frustrated with the care he was taking. It was stupid to feel that way, but true. I wanted—needed— more. So, I put my arms around his back and dug my nails into his flesh.

He cried out and thrust into me. Hard.

"Yes..." I groaned and bit into his shoulder, wrapping my legs around his waist.

"Please," I begged him. I wanted more.

I needed him to want me, to need me as I needed him. To fill the emptiness that was somehow still present.

He slid up inside of me, thrusting over and over again. I rejoiced in his body on top of mine. The weight and pressure, the feel of him against me.

I kissed his neck, his face, and he groaned. "I won't last if you keep doing that."

I didn't want him to last. I could feel Grayson in the room, hovering, waiting his turn. He would be my biggest challenge.

"Don't wait. Come inside me."

I'd never said such erotic things in my life, and I don't know if it was the primal dance or the energy in the room, but I wanted something I'd never wanted in my life.

A man's true mark on me. And I wanted to mark my men in return. I kissed Brad's neck and sunk my teeth into his skin.

He shivered violently and began to cry out. I squeezed his cock with my internal muscles and an orgasm rippled through me as his seed pulsed into me.

My body soaked up his orgasm, milked his shaft, and settled as if part of my raging need had been met. Part, but not yet all.

He groaned loudly and fell on top of me. The weight on my chest was too great and I began to pant.

"Brad, you're squishing her."

It was Grayson. His deep tone rolled over me like a warm blanket. The man who'd given me my first orgasm. Brad pushed up with his arms and I could breathe again. Phew.

"I'm so sorry, beautiful." He rolled to the side, and there he was.

The Alpha.

Stroking his long cock slowly, mesmerizing me with his action. "Come here, beautiful."

I jumped straight up and fell to my knees before him, the submissive part of me that had always wanted a man I could truly trust coming to the forefront.

I opened my mouth and he walked forward and slid his huge cock between my lips. I moaned as he took my head and gently fucked my face. He didn't force himself down my throat.

I barely had the head in my mouth, but as he thrust between my lips, my whole body relaxed. I was strangely... happy. But not sated. Quite the opposite of sated.

He gently tugged at my hair, and I pulled back to look up at him. There was no rush in Grayson's movements, no urgency. This dance was going to be a slow burn to satisfaction for both of us.

He'd waited this long, and he was going to make me wait a little longer.

"Are you too sore for me, beautiful? I can wait."

I stared up at him. He was serious. He would walk away now, even if he was hard and needing me. Having watched his two friends already have me to their end.

He'd wait. What sort of man was this?

The answer whispered itself into my mind. He's an Alpha... and a decent, kind man who protects those he cares about.

"No. Please don't make me wait."

A strange laugh chortled out of him. "Make you wait?"

He offered me his hand and lifted me to my feet. He stared down at me with all the passion and intensity I'd ever dreamed of seeing from my lover.

"Are you sure? Because you know...."

"I do." I didn't care how he was going to finish that sentence. My answer was yes. I knew he was big. I knew his passion for me would be enormous, too. And I didn't care. "I just want you."

He grinned and pressed his lips to mine in a super-sweet kiss. "You're sure?"

I nodded again and he smiled, took a breath, then stood up straighter and said,

"Get on your knees, on the bed. Present your cunt to me."

Oh. My. God.

My pussy pulsed with expectation as I turned and dove back onto the bed. On my hands and knees, like he said. Waiting for him. Waiting for possession. He didn't immediately move over to me.

I flicked my hair out of the way and looked over my shoulder at him. "What's wrong?"

"I said present. Reach back and open your cheeks for me. Show me where you want me to put my cock."

Oh. Fuuuck.

Was I really going to do that?

I dropped my head to the mattress and reached back my hands and did what he ordered me to do. I opened myself up for his perusal.

Never in my life had I been so mortified by my own behavior, yet so turned on. But I was rewarded for my bravery because Grayson set his hands on my ass cheeks, opening me up further for his cock, and set the head at my entrance.

I let go of my flesh and put my hands on the mattress once again.

He slid into me slowly, and kept going, and going. Forging inside already tender tissue until I was so full, I could barely breathe.

And yet my wanton body pushed back against him, wanting all of him.

Grayson called to his pack. "Aaron. Brad. Come and touch her."

Then I was surrounded, Brad's lips on my face, against my ear, and Aaron's hands on my back, caressing my breasts, tweaking my nipples.

All while Grayson slid his cock in and out of me, very slowly, for which I was grateful.

He was much bigger than either of the other two.

The feelings were overwhelming, in the best possible way. There were hands and lips and cocks everywhere.

My whole body was being pleasured, adored. Loved. And that's when the first orgasm suddenly hit. I screamed out as it rippled through my belly and squeezed Grayson's cock. He cried out and grabbed my hips, thrusting deeper, harder inside of me.

"Damn it, you almost dragged the cum right out of me."

Grayson's erotic words didn't stem the tide of orgasms as they began to roll over me, one after another. They wouldn't stop.

Just when I thought I could catch my breath and relax, my belly would tighten and another would roll straight through me.

And I didn't try to stop them. Nor was I silent, or quiet or lady-like. I groaned, moaned, and screamed like a wild animal.

How could I not?

"Fu...uck." Grayson began to pound into me, his fingers digging into my hips as he rode my body straight through every belly-tightening scream.

I pushed down on my hands to give Brad and Aaron full access to me and pressed back against Grayson, welcoming the heavy thumping in my belly.

They squeezed my nipples and flicked my clit, making everything so much more intense. "Grayson! Please!"

I cried out as another orgasm rolled through me and I squeezed his shaft as hard as I could.

"Oh, God! Yes, okay.... You got me. I can't hold on any longer. You better come with me, little one."

I wasn't sure I could, not again. But as the Alpha growled out his pleasure and shivering and shaking took over my whole body, I had no choice but to surrender to the power that was Grayson. Our Alpha.

I fell forward onto the bed, my body wracked with heaving spasms. Three men's bodies were around me, beside me, behind me.

And as bliss descended and exhaustion flowed through me, sleep pulled me down into blessed release.

10

———

GRAYSON

I stared down at my sleeping mate and admired every little bit of her. The shape of her spine, the curve of her ass, the sweetness of her face... Everything about her told me that I'd finally found my home.

I stretched my back, sweat covering my skin. "Whoa," I said. "That was intense."

Brad and Aaron nodded in agreement, though they didn't answer verbally. They were well on their way to falling asleep too. I, however, was nowhere near it. I still buzzed with adrenaline and the intense pleasure that had come from mating with my woman.

"You guys climb into bed and stay with her. I'm gonna have a shower."

Aaron and Brad nodded as they lifted Nevaeh up onto the pillows and pulled the covers up.

I stood frozen for several minutes, watching them, unable to move, although I itched from the sweat that stuck to my skin.

My heart was breaking. In the very best possible way. I'd never seen anything as beautiful as the sight before me. My mate,

100

nestled between my Beta and Omega. All of them sleeping soundly from the mating that would bond us all together for the rest of our lives.

I had a life, a real family, a mate. I was finally complete. I struggled with the strength of the emotions swelling in my chest.

I glanced at the door, a part of my soul wanting to shift and run. To expel all of this extra energy and race through the forest with the dirt beneath my paws and my Alpha wolf in its natural element.

But a hot shower called me, and I gave into my human side, walking into the ensuite and turning on the water.

I was tense, but full of bliss. Itchy, yet settled. I was everything all at once, and it totally blew my mind that this was where my life was now.

I stepped beneath the spray, scrubbed my skin and washed my hair. What a world this was.

Just... wow.

When I was dry and dressed again, my family finally woke.

Aaron and Brad were first to stand up and move around the room, then finally our Queen stirred. I slipped into the warm spot on the bed Aaron had left and took her, still naked, into my arms.

"How are you feeling, beautiful girl?"

She buried her head into my shoulder, her lips caressing my skin. "Good."

I chuckled. "Just good, huh? We need to try harder next time to make you feel even better, do we?"

She looked up at me, her eyes wide and scared. "I didn't mean..."

I laughed loudly. "Oh, sweetheart, I was joking."

Her smile was full of relief. "It was amazing. All of it. I've never known anything like it."

"Good! Then I hope you're going to stay here with us."

She nodded. "Yeah, I can. For a day or two, but I have to get back to work. My car needs to be fixed... I have to get back to my life."

I bit the inside of my cheek to stop from growling out loud. She wanted to get back to her life? To what? A job and an empty apartment? "Ah... all right. I suppose we can sort something out. Little River isn't far."

She sat up suddenly and slid out of bed, her gorgeously rounded ass catching my gaze while she ducked down and grabbed her clothes up off the ground.

I sat up too but stayed seated so I didn't loom over her.

"We kind of skipped lunch. Shall we go down and have something to eat?"

She smiled when she was finally clothed. "That's a good idea. I think we all worked up a bit of an appetite."

She was smiling and saying all the right things, but the stone in my gut was heavy.

Something was wrong. We hadn't done enough to get her to trust us yet, that was obvious. "Have we upset you somehow, Nevaeh?"

She walked to the bedroom door and pulled it open. "No, not at all. But I'm not quite ready to throw my whole life into chaos. Not yet, anyway. I know Claire jumped at the first chance to move in with her men, but I'm different. I'm sorry. I can't throw my life away like her."

Disbelief shot through my veins, followed quickly by anger.

Surely not...

"Is that how Claire phrases it? That she threw away her life for her mates?"

I couldn't believe it. That didn't sound like the woman next door I'd grown to know and like.

"Oh, no.... No. She's totally blissful in her ignorance."

What a horrible way to put it. Being in love was blissful ignorance?

"What's that supposed to mean?"

This conversation was getting worse by the minute. Was it possible our mate had more than a bit of shrew in her?

Nevaeh heaved a sigh and her face closed up, that cold aloofness that I'd hated seeing on her from the moment we met, returning. I couldn't believe it. Despite everything we'd shared, she was planning to leave anyway.

"Grayson, this conversation is getting out of hand. I mean... All I meant was..."

I continued to wait, staring at her intently.

She didn't finish the sentence.

Brad and Aaron came along the hallway from their bedrooms, where they'd gone to grab clean clothes, and Brad asked if we wanted lunch. Nevaeh agreed and they took off down the stairs, followed closely by Aaron, all of them laughing and chatting happily.

My head was in turmoil. What was in her mind? Should I wait and let her figure it out on her own, or push her to admit what her fears were so we could try and allay them?

I jogged down the stairs without having decided which path to take, which was never a great idea. My mom always said I was too emotional to be an Alpha. Controlling what came out of my mouth, and being patient, were not strengths of mine.

I stepped onto the landing and turned, finding our kitchen a bevy of happiness. Food preparation was underway and drinks were being poured. At the heart of it all was Nevaeh, smiling at Brad and letting Aaron drop kisses on her cheeks.

How could she possibly want to leave us?

I pushed down the need to explore that gaping hole of sadness and leaned against the couch.

Brad glanced over to me. "You gonna help?"

I laughed. "How? There's three of you in the kitchen already and with my bulk, I won't fit."

I'd get in the way, and I wasn't sure I could trust myself not to ravage her again.

Aaron grinned. "Yeah, with Nevaeh here permanently now, we should look at expanding. I know humans do extensions on their houses all the time. What do you think, beautiful?"

Nevaeh froze, but I was the only one to see it.

The others continued to smile and move around the kitchen, preparing food, oblivious to her reaction to Aaron's words.

I felt bad for everyone.

Nevaeh was obviously overwhelmed and probably feeling a little trapped, and my pack mates were about to get their balls handed to them.

I waited, my chest aching. It was like watching a car on the road, slipping and sliding amongst the elements. Knowing an accident was imminent but there was no way of stopping it.

Nevaeh moved further away, around to the side of the room. "Ah... I'm heading home later today. I have some things I need to do."

I crossed my arms and stared at her. "Didn't Claire ask you to stay for a few days, so that we could get to know each other better? Plus, I think she also made sure you had the time off work."

She glanced over to me, then back to Aaron and Brad. "Yeah, she did. But I'm not comfortable staying here tonight. Little River's only an hour away. I can come back tomorrow."

She was lying.

She won't come back tomorrow.

Brad and Aaron's faces both took on dark expressions, and the atmosphere in the room changed dramatically. The temperature dropped from comfortable to sub-arctic.

Everything in me calmed down and stilled.

"What do you mean, Nevaeh?" Aaron asked.

"What did we do wrong?" Brad queried.

Her gaze bounced between the three of us. "You didn't do anything wrong. I just need to go home. You must know what that's like. There's no place like home."

Aaron moved toward her, the pain on his face obvious. "What do you mean? You're our mate. We want this to be your home."

Nevaeh groaned and rolled her eyes, her temper catching up with her now.

"Listen... I met you guys yesterday. Yesterday! And I know you believe in this mythical fate thing, but I don't. I control what happens in my life, and you can't tell me that great sex is enough reason to rearrange your entire life."

Aaron fell away like she'd struck him and I stepped forward. Enough was enough. I had to protect my pack from the person hurting them, and at this moment, it was our mate.

"That's quite enough, Nevaeh."

She whirled on me and I was happy to take her wrath. Aaron and Brad couldn't handle Nevaeh at full tilt, I could already tell.

"What did you say to me?"

Her shock was obvious. She may have had an abusive male in the past, but she wasn't used to being spoken to like she was a child, which was what she deserved at the moment.

"I said, that's enough. You were just given the best possible gifts that all three of us could give you in bed. All the love, attention and time we have. Don't you dare tell us that you want to go home because we're just 'great sex'. You're obviously more inexperienced than I realized, otherwise you'd know that what we just shared only comes with pure intent, and love. So, if you need to go back to your life and your 'home', Nevaeh, go. But don't insult us in the process."

I held her gaze with mine and saw the spark of anger flare.

"You can't control me, Grayson. Not with sex, not with this supposed fated mate thing. You're lucky I'm still here. Because the last thing in the world that I wanted was three boyfriends with more muscles than brains."

A growl rolled through my chest and my wolf jumped to the surface. "Be careful, Nevaeh. You're crying out for a damn good spanking, so I suggest you don't push me any harder, or you'll see how dominant I can be."

Nevaeh's eyes opened like saucers. "You wouldn't."

I laughed, though there was no humor in the situation. "You've already proven that you have absolutely no taste in men and can't see the difference between a protector and a prick. So, I suggest you stop pushing to find out which one I am."

She narrowed her eyes as she shuffled like a crab, sideways around the room, toward the front door.

"No. Nevaeh. Don't go." That was Aaron, though I didn't look his way.

I kept my gaze on the woman aiming to tear our hearts from our chests.

Her eyes spat fire and I knew I was about to get another dose. "I knew it! I knew you were as bad as my ex. Thinking you can control me, own me. I'm not a fucking possession, Grayson."

This time my laugh sounded mean. Even I could hear it. "Oh, sweetheart, you have no idea what you are, or what you want. So, stop spitting and hissing at me like some sort of feral cat, and go home."

She ran to the door and threw it open, her hair flying around her in a beautiful arc.

Brad rushed forward and I grabbed his arm to stop him.

He struggled with me. "No, Grayson! You can't let her leave. We'll never find her again. We'll be alone. Forever."

I looked over to where Nevaeh was freezing up.

"Tell him he's wrong, Nevaeh. After all, Little River is only an hour away."

I gripped my Omega harder as he struggled against me. "No... Grayson. You can't..."

"I'm not doing anything, Brad. This is all on the mate who Fate sent for us. Look at her. Isn't she magnificent as she runs off and leaves us?"

My sarcastic tone reverberated through the room. Brad sighed as Nevaeh slammed the door hard enough to shake the foundations of our house.

"She's Heaven," Brad whispered.

I echoed his sigh and let him go. "Yeah, that's the twist with Heaven. You've gotta earn your way there. And the road is often fraught with pain."

11

NEVAEH

I grabbed my car keys from Claire's house, fuming with rage at Grayson and my stomach churning with emotions. Luckily, Claire was nowhere to be seen. Then I ran outside, before remembering that my car was still in the woods, broken down and bear trampled.

"Shit!" I could scream. Literally. "Argh!"

Those fucking... stupid... men! What the hell did they think I was? A possession? I looked toward the road that led out of town. Some exercise wouldn't hurt me. I picked up my cell and called the local cab service.

"Hello. Yes, my car's broken down and I'm on the river road about fifty miles out. Can you send someone? I'll be walking, and you can call me on this number. Yes. Thank you."

I started off, pounding the pavement and pumping my arms to push the blood through my body to keep me warm. I needed to cool my temper as much as keep my body heated. Hopefully, walking in the fresh air until the cab arrived, would help with both. A calmer part of my brain reminded me that the last time

I'd tried to leave this town I'd ended up in a car accident and was almost attacked by a crazed bear.

"Well, you don't have a car and it's the middle of the day still, so..." I tried to give myself a pep talk as I walked, but in fact, it wasn't exactly the middle of the day anymore. Darkness was heading over the horizon.

I walked harder. Faster. A part of me wanted to turn around and return to the safety and the warmth of Grayson's house.

No. Not again!

I was never going back to a situation where someone else could control me, belittle me, and alter my life to suit him.

But the biggest problem, if I were honest, was that I didn't trust my own judgment when it came to men.

Claire had said that the sex would show me what sort of people they were.

Oh, God, it had. Super dominant and... I couldn't even think about it... I wanted to believe they were cruel, or selfish, but that didn't fit. They had been thoughtful, and sweet, and willing to offer me the world.

But it was still hard to know what to believe. Trevor had been nice too, at the beginning. Said he loved me, gave me attention, gifts. Then the abuse started.

How could I trust Grayson not to take me down the same path? After all, he'd just shown his true colors, hadn't he? Calling me a venomous cat. Letting me leave when the others wanted me to stay.

Rejecting me.

The hot sting of tears made my eyes burn and I blinked rapidly to stem the flow. A few slipped free and made me shiver.

In walking away, I knew on a rational level that I was the one rejecting them, but it hurt that Grayson hadn't seemed to care whether I stayed or not.

I pushed the tears away and kept walking, the occasional car now driving past as I got closer to town.

I focused on my feet, the feel of the road beneath my toes. The tingle of cold on my hands. And I tried not to think about the fact that the weight of their rejection was the underlying cause of my tears.

Claire had said she'd vouch for these guys but how was that possible, when at the first sign of me asserting myself, wanting to go home, as I had every right to do, they just tossed me away?

A taxi cab drew closer, so I waved my hand and the driver pulled over beside me and rolled down his window. "You the one who called the cab?"

I nodded my head and jumped in.

"Yes. I need to get to work, please. St John's Hospital."

"Alrighty."

He did a U-turn and we drove back to town. I tried to push aside the pain that surrounded any thoughts of the pack, and the men who'd said I was their everything.

That sure hadn't lasted long.

THEY DIDN'T COME for me. Not the day after I left, nor the day after that.

Which shouldn't have surprised me. After all, men were inconsistent, fickle creatures. Weren't they? Or was that women?

I couldn't tell anymore.

But every day I was away from them, my heart hurt.

My throat ached.

And I wasn't battling a cold. I was sure of it. My head thumped with a headache and I had chills while I slept.

"Good night, Nevaeh," my supervisor called out as I headed

for the exit after my shift. I was back at work, doing what I loved. So why wasn't I happier about it?

"Night, Trish."

It was cold and dark, and I couldn't wait to get home.

Home.

What a strange concept now.

I'd busted my butt, and Grayson's, to come home to an apartment I shared with a girl I barely knew. It was old, and untidy, and not at all what I wanted for my home.

But I was making do, as I always did. Until I reached my goal.

Enough money to own a house for myself.

I called an uber and walked up the stairs to the apartment, my heart heavy and tears on the tips of my lashes.

Damn it. Pull yourself together.

"Sophie?" I called out as I pushed open the door. She should be home at this time of night.

When Sophie didn't respond, I locked the door, flicked on the lights and moved into the kitchen. She could be asleep. We kept odd hours with our shifts at the hospital, but it would have been nice to have someone to talk to when I got home.

Maybe I should call Claire and ask how she was going; how they were doing.

No, that would be stupid. And probably unwelcome. I could only imagine what Grayson and the others had told her about me.

"Hello, Angel."

I froze. That voice was at the center of my nightmares.

There was a man in my dining room. He was not welcome within a hundred feet of me. He was not wanted, and least of all, was he permitted in my home.

I turned slowly, my eyes flicking toward the knife block in the kitchen. I had to be careful not to make any sudden moves because Trevor, despite his massive size, was as fast as a whip.

"Trevor... what are you doing here?"

He'd changed in the months I hadn't seen him. His hair was long and bedraggled. He looked like he hadn't showered in weeks.

"I've come to see my girl. I don't know why you keep avoiding me."

I shivered, the cold dread of disgust curling in my belly. I forced myself to stay calm, though my heart hammered my lungs like a blacksmith working an anvil.

"Avoiding you? Trevor, we broke up years ago. I've been getting on with my life."

"Oh, really? And what life is that, Heaven?"

His tone made me shudder and brought back so many terrible memories of times he'd called me that. Times we'd had sex... times he'd hit me. Every memory related to him was disgusting to me.

Where was my phone? If I could get away from him, I could call the police. That wasn't going to be easy inside our small apartment.

Damn it... What could I do?

I went about unpacking my bag on the counter as casually as I could, considering my heart was pounding in my chest. I pulled out my water bottle, my lunch box. I washed them both out in the kitchen sink, moving slowly and steadily.

I injected as much humor as possible into my tone. "You know what I'm like. Work, work, work."

He laughed, too, but the sound was ugly and cruel. "Oh, I do know you, and you're a little slut is what you are. Going for three men at once. Tut tut tut." He tsked at me and I knew my time had come.

He was about to increase the pressure. I took my cell phone from my backpack and slid it into my back pocket. "I didn't..."

"Oh, yes you did."

He stood up and I began to panic. Adrenaline raced along my veins, making my arms shake.

He grunted and raised his voice. "I can smell them on you! You should have listened to me! I tried to warn you the other night, in the forest."

I walked toward the door but kept my gaze on Trevor so he didn't know I was about to bolt. "That was you? In the woods? The bear?"

I'd assumed it was him, of course. But to know it was him, now that was a different story.

Trevor puffed up like an arrogant peacock. "Of course, it was me. You know I have bear shifter genes."

"You could have killed me."

He growled, low and menacing. "No... I didn't want that. But you do need protecting. I can't have you mating with those wolves. That pack's destiny is to die out."

I stilled. "What do you mean? What destiny?"

He laughed and moved closer, so I walked away from my potential exit to keep him talking. I circled the island bench.

"Tell me, Trevor. They all said I was their... mate. But I didn't believe them."

He grinned. "That's my girl."

He didn't give me any more information and a part of me ached to know more. To ferret out the truth. "Is that why you chose me, Trevor?"

I'd always wondered why a guy who seemed to hate me, professed to love me.

"I could smell it on you... you know? That wolfy, magical shit. Smells disgusting." He spat on the ground, on my tiled floor, and kept following me in the circle around the bench.

A dangerous dance. "Then why date me, Trevor?"

"To keep the wolves off you. To make you smell like me. They'd never go for you if they could smell bear on your pussy."

He grinned, that terrible expression of humor that I'd always hated.

"So... let me get this straight. You could tell that I was meant to be a wolf shifter's mate, so you... what? Deliberately sabotaged their plans?"

He growled again and I jumped.

"I didn't want to," he said. "My father, our Alpha, demanded it. Those wolves are meant to die out. Their bloodlines aren't meant to continue. There have been no female shifters born in generations. Fate chose it for them. You humans aren't allowed to step in and contradict Fate."

I held up my hand and he stopped moving closer. "Hang on a second. You think Fate's trying to wipe them out? Then why create a human fated mate at all? And what do you care about me now, anyway? They've got Claire, so their line will continue, no matter what. And they'll find more of us. Why try and stop me from going to them?"

This didn't make any sense to anyone except this idiot before me. That was when his malicious grin skittered across his face. The one that told me to run.

"Because you're mine. And if I can't have you, no one can."

I ran. Straight to the only room in the house with a lock. The bathroom. I bolted inside, the pounding of his footsteps behind me on the tiles echoing everywhere.

I slammed the door and locked it, but that wouldn't hold him for long. So, I sat on the ground, with my back against the door and pushed my legs against the bathtub to leverage my weight.

It was all I could do. There was nothing else to move, or put in front of the door.

"Open the door! Now!" Trevor bellowed.

I grabbed my phone out of my back pocket and that was when I saw a very recent message from an unknown cell number.

Are you okay?

Tears sprung to my eyes as I hit dial on the number. Only three people in the world could feel my panic, and that had to be my soul mate shifters.

The phone rang once and then Grayson answered. "Nevaeh. Are you all right?"

"No! Trevor's here—at my apartment. He's trying to hurt me!"

"We're on our way."

"Ninety-nine Shalloway Street, Apartment Three. You'll hear the.... screaming. Fuck!"

Trevor slammed his weight against the door and pain shot down my spine.

"Call the police," Grayson yelled. "We'll be there soon."

He hung up and I called nine-one-one. "Oh, please... please hurry," I begged, when I got through.

Trevor must have run at the door with all his strength, because the next thing I knew, my ankle gave way, pain shot through my skull, and the whole world went black.

12

GRAYSON

The night air flew past my face as we ran through the forest at break-neck speed. Aaron was at my right. Brad had gone to Dex for extra help, so hopefully the other pack was close behind us.

My thoughts were jumbled, angry screams as we ran as fast as we could, straight toward town. We could sense that Nevaeh was hurt, but how badly?

If he hit her again, that ex- boyfriend was going to die. And if he'd done worse... well then, he'd die slowly.

My paws hit the dirt and propelled me through the forest until we reached the outskirts of town. Aaron had matched my breakneck pace and was still at my side.

It was past midnight, so luckily there weren't many people out and about to freak out about two wolves running through the town. We turned the corner and kept going. I used my connection to Nevaeh to guide us in the right direction to her apartment. I could scent that it was close, but I couldn't sense Nevaeh's presence nearby.

Where was our mate? We took the next left and saw her

street name. Thank God, we were almost there. We found the apartment and pushed into the open door.

I shifted back into human form and so did Aaron, sweat dripping down our burning hot skin.

"Where. Is. She?" Aaron panted, our bodies close to exhaustion already.

"I don't know. Nevaeh! Nevaeh!"

We ran through the apartment, the smell of fear and bear permeating my senses. "Fuck. He's a bear. The ex. It must have been him. The one who knocked over her car that night."

That made sense, of course, but I'd hoped the logical conclusion wasn't the correct one.

"Where did he take her, then?" Aaron asked, looking around the tiny apartment but not seeing any clue. I couldn't sense her at all, now.

"I don't know. But we need to find them."

A car screeched to a halt at the front of the apartment, and I raced to the window.

"It's Dex and Brad," I called over my shoulder to Aaron. "Let's go."

There were two trucks out the front. They were barely minutes behind us and they weren't exhausted. We jogged down the stairs, naked and cooling down.

"Maybe we should have brought the car?" Aaron said, his tone full of sarcasm and wry humor.

I glanced at him. "Did you think about that when you found out Nevaeh was in trouble?"

Aaron shook his head. "Nope. My wolf took over and I was running beside you before I'd even decided to shift."

That's exactly what had happened to me. "Yeah. I know the feeling. Let's go."

We jogged outside and Brad tossed a pair of jeans at each of us.

"Get in, guys. From the smell of this place, we have a bear to hunt." Dexter gestured to the second car.

We jumped into the vehicle Brad was driving and Dexter jumped out, stripping to his birthday suit.

"I'm gonna shift and follow the scent. You guys drive behind me. Save your strength. There's going to be a fight at the end of this. I can feel it already."

Dexter shifted into his massive, silver, Alpha wolf and I drank the bottle of water Brad put in front of me.

He was right. Aaron and I were tired from the frantic dash here, and if we were going up against a den of bears, then we were going to need all our strength, or at least, as much as we could recoup in the time it took to find our mate.

Dexter took off and we drove after him, through the town. He stopped at different spots, sniffing the air, different vehicles. Doors.

I could smell the bear too... and then something else. Someone else. Someone sweet.

"That's Nevaeh," Aaron said through growling teeth.

I nodded, unable to speak. My wolf rose to the surface, wanting to run, fight, protect my mate. Even though she'd left us, run away from her destiny, I wanted her.

The cars pulled over and we jumped out, heading over to Dex, as he shifted and stood in his human form.

"The scent of the bear ends here. Maybe one of you guys can pick up Nevaeh's scent instead?"

Brad stripped off his jacket and threw it at me. He peeled off the rest of his clothing in record time. "My turn."

Brad's human form disappeared, and his brown wolf stepped up to us, lifted his head and sniffed the air. Then he turned and started running.

I hesitated for a moment. My wolf wanted to run with my

Omega, lead my pack as an Alpha should. But it was time to work together and use our brains as well as our raw instincts.

I jumped back into the car with Aaron and we took off, through the other side of the city and into the woods once again. Heading in the opposite direction of our pack.

We were on our own if things went pear-shaped out this way.

We drove deeper into the forest, no longer on actual roads, feeling our way along dirt paths. Following Brad. Then a shotgun sounded in the quiet of the night and Aaron slammed on the brakes.

Brad dropped to the ground.

"Brad! No!"

I jumped up and shifted, racing straight to Brad, grabbing him by the scruff of the neck and pulling him behind the cars. The gun boomed again somewhere over my head but I kept dragging. I had to get my pack mate to safety.

I shifted back once we were safe, and Dexter came over to check him out.

Brad was still breathing, but only just. "He needs the hospital. Now."

He wasn't shifting back, which was a bad sign. He had a gunshot wound in his hindquarters and I knew he'd likely require surgery.

Jay, Dexter's Omega, stepped up. "I'll take him and call Claire on the way. Get him into the car."

Dexter nodded. "Yes. Perfect plan. We'll stay and help you guys."

We lifted my Omega into one of the cars and Jay took off.

"God, I hope he's okay," Aaron said.

I nodded, too worried to answer out loud. Another gunshot blasted next to the remaining car and we jumped behind it.

Dexter groaned. "He'll be fine, I'm sure. But we've gotta stay alive long enough to visit him in the hospital. So, what's the plan?"

I crouched down with the other Alpha and our Betas. "We go in, save my mate, and kill anyone who gets in our way."

The other three wolf shifters nodded, and we turned to assess the best way to take the cottage. Because somewhere inside that small house was my mate, and I wasn't going home without her.

13

NEVAEH

Blood dripped down my nose, making my lips taste of metallic salt. *Yuck.* My right eye was swollen shut, and I was tied to a chair in the middle of some backwoods cabin, but there was nothing wrong with my hearing.

For the past God knows how long, Trevor had been fighting with an older man who sounded very similar to Trevor.

His father, probably. And they were arguing over what to do with me. Trevor didn't want his dad to hurt me, but he didn't want to keep me, either. The guy really didn't know what he wanted. Not at all.

And although I should be terrified, and a part of me was, somehow I knew my mates would come for me. I could hear the two men moving around. All I could think was, what was going to happen when my mates arrived?

Would they get hurt?

What if it was Brad who arrived? Would he be strong enough to take on two bear shifters? My heart just about tore apart thinking about it, until I couldn't breathe for the pain it caused me.

My men...

The people I'd run away from, rejected and decided I couldn't possibly live with. They'd come for me. They'd save me. I knew they would. Because they thought I belonged with them. And now, as my head throbbed with pain and my hands were bound behind my back, I called myself ten kinds of fool for running away.

Why was I so scared?? Because it was too perfect?

Because I'd had too many orgasms?

Because I was too chicken-shit scared to love someone?

Yes, it was the latter, for sure. Because loving someone meant really trusting them. And I had trust issues.

Obviously.

"Fuck! There they are! Get your shotgun and give it to me." The older man stomped around the room, and I tried not to move and draw his attention, though I was so uncomfortable I could barely refrain from wriggling around to find a position that hurt less.

Slowly, I lifted my head and opened the eye that was not swollen shut.

The older man was definitely Trevor's dad, if his physique and receding hairline were to be believed.

He lifted the weapon that Trevor handed him and said the best thing I'd heard all day.

"Fucking wolf shifters."

Then the gun went off and I cried out, my heart pummeling into my ribs as adrenaline raced through my veins.

Trevor ran over to me. "They're not going to rescue you, you stupid little bitch. You were mine first."

He yanked at my arms, and it felt like he was untying me. Then I was on my feet and hauled to the front door.

"What's happening? I can't see," I whispered, leaning against

Trevor as though I didn't even have the strength to stand on my own.

I did, though. And I could run if the need rose.

"They're leaving. Ha! Your wolves are cowards. Look at them run."

"What's happening, Trevor? Tell me," I whispered.

He chuckled and I relaxed into him even more.

I didn't care what he did to me today, as long as I was alive at the end of it and could tell all three of my mates I was sorry for running.

"We shot the little brown wolf."

My heart skipped a beat. Little brown wolf? Brad? Was he alive?

"They're taking him away... hang on. Shit. The other four are still here. That's two Alphas and their Betas. Dad, we can't take on all four of them."

"Oh, yes, we can. You shift and attack the Alpha and I'll be right behind you with the shotgun. It's time we got rid of this whole pack."

I held my breath, waiting for them to decide what to do with me. Trevor seemed to think me inconsequential, because he tossed me aside and strode out the front door. Pain shot through my elbow and my leg as I landed on the floor.

The older man chuckled. "I wish he hadn't hit you quite so hard, girly. This is something you'll want to see."

I didn't want to see anything happen to my wolf shifter men. But I couldn't help myself from looking anyway. I dragged myself slowly across the floor to the window and managed to pull up to a stand.

My whole body ached, but as my one eye that worked focused on my men stalking toward the cottage, my pain disappeared, and fear consumed me.

My throat closed up and an invisible band pressed against my ribs. They'd come to save me. They hadn't rejected me, nor abandoned me. They were here for me, when I most needed them.

When had anyone else in my entire life been able to be counted on like that? Tears blinded me and I sniffed loudly, wiping my face with my sleeve.

A growl rolled through the clearing as Trevor pulled off his shirt and his soft, but very large body transformed into an eight-foot-tall, ferocious-looking black bear.

The old man in the cabin with me said, "Okay, Alpha. You're going down."

I had to save them. I screamed out as loudly as I could, "Grayson! Watch out!"

The shotgun blasted beside me, and I fell sideways, away from the sound and the man who shoved me. Trevor's father growled and began to tug at his own clothes.

He was going to shift, it seemed, and that wasn't something I was hanging around for. When he opened the front door and ran outside, beginning to transform, I realized that was the only chance I'd get to escape.

I staggered to my feet, scrabbling over the dirt littering the floor, and my own painful injuries, and ran the other way through the house, wrenching open the back door and stumbling out into the forest.

I started to run, then heard a howl.

A wolf. Hurt.

I stopped running and turned back. I couldn't abandon them now. Not that they'd see it that way, I was sure. But I had to help, somehow. Only, how?

The gun!

I raced back inside the cabin and grabbed the shotgun from where it had fallen to the floor.

My parents were classic trailer trash, and they loved their

guns. I hadn't fired one since I was a teenager. But I knew how to load one, and God help me, I knew how to shoot straight.

I hit the barrel breach lever, checking for shells.

Empty.

I stared around the room for the box, forcing my one eye to focus despite the stress. I felt for them, checking the shelves, the drawers in the table.

"Yes!"

There was a red box in the bottom drawer, full of shotgun shells. There was a flurry of noise outside. I looked through the window.

The fight was vicious and from my vantage point it looked like the bears were winning, somehow. My men needed me.

I loaded the gun quickly and slid extra shells into my back pocket.

I walked out onto the front step and leveled the gun at one of the black bears—the one who had his jaw clamped around the black wolf beneath him.

I lifted the gun and set it right in my shoulder, sighted with my one working eye, and squeezed the trigger.

Bulls eye.

Or in this case, bear's eye. Sort of. I'd hit him, but not anywhere that would kill him.

The bear released the wolf and staggered sideways. Then he turned on me. His slobbering, saliva-covered mouth opened to reveal a mass of sharp teeth.

He charged at me.

I raised the gun again and fired directly into his face. Then I closed my eyes and waited for the impact. None came. I opened my good eye and looked down.

He was sprawled at my feet, a dead four-hundred-pound animal. In death, the bear remained a bear... which surprised me.

Why wouldn't he turn back into a human?

Then I heard the blood-curdling screams of his son, still in bear form. Larger than his father. And completely and utterly enraged.

Trevor dropped to all fours and charged me.

I found the lever on the break action, quickly expelled the shells and reached into my back pocket for two more rounds. If I didn't reload quickly, it would be too late for me.

"Shit!"

I pulled them out, then dropped one. My hands were shaking too hard.

And then he was nearly on me. As I opened my mouth to scream, a massive silver wolf jumped in front of me, his growl making the hairs on my neck stand up. He launched himself at the bear, tearing at his throat.

Then another silver wolf attacked too, jumping in to support the first wolf, taking out the bear's legs and sending him to the ground. I grabbed again for the shells, my hands trembling so much I could barely re-load. But finally, I managed it.

I held up the shotgun.

The bear suddenly began to shift back to human form—back to Trevor—his bleeding body heaving with exertion.

The wolves shifted back too, obviously assuming the threat was over.

I wasn't so sure, and kept the gun relaxed, but in my hands, ready to lift and fire if he so much as threatened any of my mates.

My mates... Damn, how the tables had turned.

"What's wrong, Trevor? Lost the fight and want to surrender?" I asked, my tone goading as I stood there with my battered body.

But I was still standing.

"No. I wanted to see the look on these guys' faces when they saw my marks on you. Isn't she beautiful like that, boys?" he asked, gesturing to my face.

"Why, you..." Aaron dove for him, and Trevor, fast as lightning, got Aaron in a headlock and began backing away.

Aaron tapped his arms, struggling in Trevor's grip, but he was gasping for air.

"Drop the gun or I'm going to break his neck."

Grayson danced on his toes like a boxer about to go into the ring.

"Let him go, you coward," Grayson said. "You know I'm the one you want. Come on. Alpha on Alpha."

Trevor laughed and tightened his grip on Aaron's throat.

I didn't want this. I didn't want any of my men hurt, and Aaron was turning blue.

I yelled out to the man I hated. "Take the car and go. Get out of here. Grayson, throw Trevor your keys."

"Drop the gun," he demanded again, and this time I placed it on the ground.

"There. Now let Aaron go."

"Keys," he grunted.

Grayson hesitated. "They're in the car."

Aaron was drooping, his eyelids fluttering as he began to lose consciousness.

"Trevor! You won, let him go! Now!"

Trevor dragged Aaron the few more feet to the car, then threw him to the ground. He lay there unmoving, as Trevor jumped into the car and revved the engine. He yelled out, "Thanks for the final fuck, baby. You were smokin' hot!"

I would have rolled my eyes at the ridiculous statement if I wasn't so worried about Aaron. I hurried over to him while Trevor sped away. I moved Aaron onto his side and made sure his airway was clear.

He was breathing on his own, thank God, and would likely come back to us in a few moments, though his throat looked bruised, and he'd be sore when he woke up.

"I should chase him down and kill him for what he did to you," Grayson said, though I could see he was torn whether to leave us.

I played on that indecision. "I know. But we need you here, Grayson. What if other bear shifters come and attack?"

Grayson nodded, and for the first time I noticed his nakedness.

And Dexter's... oh, and Taylor's, too. Damn. Naked men everywhere.

"Ah..." My cheeks were hot with embarrassment. I looked down again at Aaron. "How are we going to get out of here now?"

Aaron woke up slowly and groaned. "Nevaeh... God, what did he do to your face?"

I sat down on the ground, wincing as I did, pulling Aaron's head into my lap. "Nothing he hasn't done before."

Dexter and Taylor stepped close in human form and even though their nude bodies didn't make me react inside the way Grayson and Aaron's did, I couldn't help noticing that Claire was as lucky as I was in that department.

"We'll go," Dex said. "Find a car and come back to you. If you're lucky, though, Jay may get back here first. He'll likely return from the hospital to check on us once he's dropped Brad off."

Grayson shook hands with the other Alpha. "Thanks, Dex. We'll be here waiting for you."

Dexter and Taylor shifted into incredibly beautiful silver and black wolves and took off.

"Whoa, that's incredible."

Grayson squatted down beside me. "Why aren't you more freaked out with us shifting? Dexter said Claire practically had a heart attack the first time she saw them do it."

I swallowed hard. "Well, I'd seen Trevor shift once before.

Years ago. But he threatened me and told me he'd kill me if I ever told anyone."

"Uh huh." Grayson sounded as though he didn't believe me.

"It's true, Grayson. I promise."

He looked me straight in the eyes. "Well, sweetheart, I think we have a lot to talk about, don't you?"

I nodded, a sinking feeling hitting my stomach.

Aaron's eyes closed from fatigue, and I stroked his thick hair and tried to relax, until a car pulled up to take us to the hospital and find out if Brad was all right.

14

BRAD

I opened my eyes to the sounds and bright lights of hospital. Why was I in a hospital?

"He's awake."

Nevaeh was beside the bed, holding my hand and staring at me like she'd never seen me before. One of her eyes was swollen shut and I could see she was in a lot of pain.

"Hey, beautiful... what happened?" I couldn't pull my mind together long enough to put the pieces together.

"You got shot."

I glanced down at my white sheet-covered body and although I couldn't see the injury, I could feel it. The ache in my leg. "Oh... great. How long have I been out?"

"Only a few hours," Grayson said from the other side of the bed.

"What happened?" I grabbed Nevaeh's hand and squeezed, hard. "I don't like to see you hurt."

She gave me a small smile. "I'm okay, now you're awake. Trevor's dad shot you. There were shell fragments lodged inside your quadriceps muscle, but one of the surgeons managed to extract them." She lowered her voice. "We told them it was a hunting accident."

I wanted to laugh, but instead my heart ached at how loving our mate was. "No, beautiful. I meant you. What happened to you?"

"Oh..." She drew back her hand and pulled her fingers through her hair, glancing down as though she were embarrassed. "Ah..."

"He beat her up," Grayson growled out. "And for that, we're going to kill him."

"No, please, don't," Nevaeh said. "I don't want anything bad to happen to you. None of this matters, as long as the three of you are okay."

Grayson stared at her. "You care about us now, do you?"

"Of course. You know I do."

Aaron laughed. "How would we know that?"

Nevaeh sighed. "I... I... can we do this later? When Brad and I are better?"

Aaron and Grayson nodded.

I sighed. They knew we all belonged together. "How long do I have to stay here?" I asked her, grabbing Nevaeh's hand again.

"Well, usually it would be a few days to a week. But Grayson said you guys heal very quickly, so I don't know."

I flexed my foot and bent my knee. It hurt, but nothing I hadn't dealt with before.

"I can probably go home today, sweetheart. Another few hours and I'll be strong enough. Can you go tell the doctors? I need to talk to Grayson and Aaron."

She nodded and left the small cubicle.

I pinned my Alpha with a stare. "What the fuck happened out there? One minute we're pulling up, ready to save our mate, then I get shot and wake up here. What did I miss? You said we're going to kill him. That means you didn't kill that asshole yet?"

"No. We couldn't." Grayson's gaze slid to Aaron. "He had Aaron round the throat, and if we didn't let the bastard leave, he was going to kill him."

Aaron's face reddened and he looked away, then crossed his arms over his chest. "Not sure you made the right choice there."

"Of course, I did," Grayson said, his tone deep and growly. "I'm just angry the bear got away."

"And what happened with Nevaeh? Why is there so much tension? I could slice it off with a knife."

"I don't think that's the expression," Aaron said.

I raised my eyebrows and stared at him. "Oh, seriously?" He must be really embarrassed by what had happened out there if he was trying to make jokes like that.

Grayson took a step toward the door. "Now that we know you're all right, we'll go home for a bit. I need a shower and some sleep. But we'll come back to pick you up when they say we can take you home."

"Hang on, you didn't tell me what happened with Nevaeh." The woman in question stepped into the room.

"We'll let her tell you," Grayson said, before disappearing from sight.

Aaron nodded once and left too.

Nevaeh was left swaying like a leaf in the wind, looking lost and confused. I grabbed her hand and tugged her back into the chair next to my hospital bed. "Hey, beautiful. Seems like I've missed a few things. What's going on?"

Nevaeh clung to my hand. "I don't really know. I mean... I know I left your place in a huff the other day, which was wrong and stupid, but when you three turned up to save me, I assumed you'd be happy to see me. But Aaron and Grayson are standoffish and angry. I mean... I know I stuffed up, but I..."

She stopped.

"You what, sweetheart?"

"I was hoping we could sort everything out, but it looks like they're not going to forgive me for my stupidity." Silvery tears slipped down her cheeks and she wiped her nose with a Kleenex from the table by my bed.

"Oh, sweetheart. Why are you upset? You haven't even asked a question of anyone. We came for you. We fought for you."

Well, Aaron and Grayson had. I'd have fought for her too, if I hadn't been shot.

Nevaeh stood up and moved away, swiping at the tears. "Oh... I'm not... I..."

I stared at her. Did she assume we'd rejected her? Chasing our mate was part of our very DNA. Did she not know that? But at the same time, we also needed to know that she wanted us, too. That she hadn't permanently rejected us.

"I need to go, Brad. But I'll be back later."

"Sweetheart, let me say one more thing before you run away. I know that we are a lot to take. Three of us claiming you're our mate, the whole wolf thing... but we want you. All of you. We want to love you. But we won't force you to be with us. So, if you want to try again, or at least give us another chance to see if this relationship will work... assuming you do...?"

She nodded quickly and relief winged through my heart. Thank the heavens for that. "Then perhaps you should say something—or do something, to let us all know. Aaron and Grayson just threw themselves in front of guns and crazed bears for you."

"So did you," she whispered.

"Of course, I did. You're my mate."

She nodded and practically ran out the door.

"Oh... shit." I scrubbed my face with my hands. What a mess.

～

During my dinner, Grayson and Aaron turned up in my hospital room once again. I was forcing down the food with a fork made of plastic. Disgusting. But I was hungry.

"Let's go, Brad. It's getting dark and we want to be home at a decent hour."

I threw back the sheet and swung my legs over the edge of the bed. I was moving a lot better now. The difference of a few hours. "Great. Let's go."

The nurse wheeled in a wheelchair, a grim look on her face. "We don't advise this, Mr. Thompson. It's too soon after surgery to be leaving the hospital."

I smiled at her. For a human it probably was too early, but I was ready. "Thanks for all the help today, but I'm pretty right. We heal fast in my family."

I stood up, grimacing as pain shot through my thigh and made a liar of me. Okay, so I was on the mend, but not quite there yet. "I'll be right to walk."

She rolled her eyes at me. "Absolutely not. It's hospital policy. Get in." She pointed to the wheelchair.

I looked at Grayson, the big powerful Alpha, who was grinning his head off.

"Shut up," I warned him, before turning to sit my ass in the bloody wheelchair.

Aaron laughed, loudly.

"Asshole," I muttered. I was wheeled out of the tiny room, into the stark hallway and out big, double doors.

The clean air on my face was one of the best moments I'd had today. I pushed up out of the chair and stood up.

"Thank you, Nurse Melanie."

She huffed and puffed and pushed the chair back into the hospital.

Grayson dangled his car keys and opened the door to his black car. "Get in, you poor sick dude."

I did get in, somehow. I sat in the back seat and put my leg over the other two seats. The others got in and we started driving back to Woodlands territory.

I sighed, my heart aching for my mate. "I can't believe we're going home without Nevaeh."

Silence.

Were they going to ignore me? "Seriously guys, what the hell happened after I got shot? Did Nevaeh shout to the world that she'd never love us, or something?"

Grayson stayed silent. Stoic. His normal strong, stubborn self.

I turned my attention to Aaron. "Come on, Aaron. Tell me. What happened with the bears?"

Aaron huffed and sighed for a bit. But I had time. It was an hour's drive home. They wouldn't make the distance if I kept poking and prodding at them.

After a few more minutes, Aaron broke. "Okay, fine. Basically, we fought the bears, we killed the older one... or Nevaeh did, actually. She shot it dead. Then the younger one... Nevaeh's ex, shifted back. We..." He sighed. "Got sucked into shifting back too. Idiot that I am. And he grabbed me."

Everything started to fall into place. Their pride had been hurt. They were angry and upset.

"So, he used you to get away. What happened after that? Why is Nevaeh's face all smashed up like that?"

Aaron looked out the window. "He did it before we got there. And we don't know what else he did, because she wouldn't talk to us. Or look at us. Or..."

I waited, and no one continued to talk.

"So, hang on. We had, like, the fight of our lives, which I missed—and our mate walked away—beaten up, but still alive. And you just... what? Let her go?"

Grayson finally grunted and said. "Look, we didn't let her go. She ran... literally ran away from us. Even after she'd been attacked in the woods that first time, in her car, she…. she decided she'd rather walk all the way home, than be with us. What does that say about her? About us! About our mating and our love-making ability. Fuck, Brad, I give up. Okay? I can't…."

Grayson broke off, and for the first time in the ten years since we'd become a family, I knew he was broken. She'd broken him. And she was the only one who could re-build him into the Alpha he was meant to become.

I stayed silent for the rest of the drive, secure in the idea that our mate was ours. That we'd touched her heart as deeply as she'd touched ours.

She was as broken without us, as we were without her.

She'd come for us.

If it wasn't today, it would be tomorrow. And if it wasn't tomorrow… I'd bite my own ass.

15

NEVAEH

My hands shook as I pushed open the front door and watched the boys' car pull up. I'd been at their place for over two hours already, timed by Claire to give me maximum time in the house without them.

After my talk with Brad, I'd realized he was right and that I needed to do something to show them how sorry I was for walking away. I'd called Claire and we formulated a plan for me to show them how much I wanted to be with them.

I'd brought my clothes, my knick-knacks, my tampons and my food. They were about to get me hard, fast, and perfume clouded. All of me, Brad had said. The three of them wanted all of me.

Well, I was about to find out if they were telling the truth. This had to be the biggest, scariest moment of my life.

I waved from the door as the men got out of the car. They stopped when they saw me, looking stunned, then started forward.

I'd iced my injuries and was dosed up on anti-inflammatories and pain meds. No way did I look too pretty now, but I wasn't feeling any pain. I smiled, though my heartbeat so fast I was terrified I was going to throw up in front of them all and ruin my classy reunion.

I didn't cook, but I had organized take-out. Lots of it. And the house smelled like hot apple pie, Thai noodles and pizza. "Hey. Welcome home."

Grayson walked up to the door first, his lips ticking up at the sides in a smile, so we were off to a good start. He wasn't kicking me out, which I had worried was a real possibility after the way he spoken to me today at the hospital.

He shoved his hands into his pockets and rolled his shoulders forward like an awkward teenager. God, he was beautiful. So strong, and yet so shy.

Aaron walked up next. His chin stuck out and his eyes looked guarded. He wasn't smiling, but at least he didn't scowl at me.

Brad limped up last, a big grin on his face. At least one of them was happy to see me. They lined up, all three of them. Staring at me. And although my belly quivered with nerves and fear that they might reject me, my heart sung with happiness to see them all here and in one piece.

I'd never known these feelings existed until a few days ago. This clawing need to be close to them was almost overwhelming.

"Hey, beautiful." Brad said, then grimaced.

What? Oh, shit. His leg! "Come in, so sorry! You should be sitting down, Brad."

I rushed forward and moved right in beside him, letting him lean on me.

"I'm okay." He laughed "You go in and fluff the pillows."

He pushed me forward and I did as he directed. Ran inside and moved the pillows around and got a chair from the kitchen so that Brad could elevate his leg easily.

"What's that smell?" he asked with another big grin as he hobbled inside and set himself up on the couch where I'd arranged everything for him.

Grayson and Aaron followed, but they didn't speak and I began to worry.

"It's, ah... I brought some dinner. I wasn't sure what you guys like, so I got a little of everything."

Brad took my hand and pulled me down next to him. "I'm starved after a day on that hospital food. Grab me some pizza, would ya?"

I did. I grabbed one of the three boxes and brought it over to the couch. Aaron and Grayson continued to stand near the door. I swallowed hard and turned to study them. They were looking around the room, probably noticing the little things I'd brought with me.

"Are you guys hungry too? Can I get you something?"

Grayson sighed. "What's this about, Nevaeh?"

"I told you. I wanted to bring you dinner, but... you should know, I don't cook."

Aaron glared at me. "We don't need you to cook. We're not looking for a housekeeper. We've gotten along very well without you for all these years."

Nerves hit me and I swallowed hard.

I should have known this wasn't going to be easy, but I hadn't thought my courage would desert me so quickly. "Okay..."

Grayson put out a hand as though to stop Aaron's words. "Nevaeh, why are you here?"

Panic bounced down my spine with the force of a bowling ball. "Because I want to be here... with you all."

"Do you, now? Since when?" Grayson crossed his arms over his chest, and I had an overwhelming urge to fall to my knees and service him. But there was so much more to be said.

"Since... the moment I left." I looked around the room, trying to connect with them all at once. "I'm so sorry I ran out on you the other day. I... behaved badly. I was scared, and overwhelmed, and I over-reacted."

Aaron walked closer; his aura softening for the first time. "What's there to be afraid of?"

I laughed, tears filling my eyes. "Are you kidding me? Everything. How I feel about you guys, what it will mean for my life. What I'll lose. What I'll gain. I'm terrified."

I laughed and hiccupped and wiped away the tears as they fell. *Fuck it. I'm all in.*

"Look, ah... this is me. I'm a mess. I came here today to tell you I want to try to be what you want me to be. I'll move in, give you everything that I am, but you have to know... I'm not perfect. Nowhere near it. I'm totally broken... a mess... with a shit past. But if you still want me after all that." I spread my arms wide out in front of me. "Then I'm all yours."

Grayson stepped around me. "Sit. We're going to sort this out."

I felt awkward, but I stayed standing in front of them like I was giving a sermon. Or a confession. Or both. "Ah..." How did I even start?

Grayson grunted. "Now, tell me what all this crap is about?"

I looked up at him, and sighed, the tension of the last few days getting to me. I was uncomfortable, nervous, scared and hopeful all wrapped up in one.

"I told you already."

"Yeah, you said you're a mess. Explain that to us."

God... where did I begin? "Well, for starters, I can't cook. I grew up with nothing, so I have trailer park parents and an obsession for trinkets, so I collect everything. I'm a major hoarder. You may need to extend the house just for that issue alone." I took a shaky breath.

"I'm a girl, so there will be makeup and bras and tampons all over the house and bathroom. I am not a neat person." My chest heaved with the stress of revealing everything.

Brad and Aaron looked at each other but Grayson was staring

at me. "And? You think we'll fear your feminine products? Are you serious right now?"

He sounded offended, and that wasn't what I was hoping for at all.

"It's not just that. I'm bad news! Look what happened yesterday with the bears. That asshole came after me because I'm your mate and he deliberately baited you! If I wasn't around, he would never have hurt you guys."

Grayson held up a hand. "Hold up. What did you just say?"

"Um... Which part?"

"About the bears. Did they say something to you, about you being our mate?"

I nodded. Hadn't I told them this part yet? Probably not, because I hadn't seen them all together since we'd visited Brad at the hospital directly after Trevor ran off.

"Yeah. Sorry—I meant to tell you that part, but so much had happened. Anyway, Trevor told me that he didn't really want to date me all those years ago, but he could tell from the smell of me that I was a wolf shifter's mate. And the bears believe you guys are meant to die out... or something like that. So, they figured that if they kept me away from you, then your line would expire."

The room was so quiet you could have heard the proverbial pin drop.

Aaron sat forward on the couch. "Are you telling us that the bears can tell who our mates are, and are deliberately keeping them from us?"

They were horrified, that was clear.

I nodded. "Yes. That's what Trevor said."

Brad groaned. "Oh, that's fucked up. Here we are, like, dying of loneliness, and they're... what...."

The mood in the room had shifted. They were angry and upset, but it wasn't directed at me, and that gave me a nice break. I took a breath while they discussed what they'd tell the pack.

I walked to the kitchen and grabbed a chair, dragging it into the living room so that I could sit across from them. But as soon as I sat down, they swiveled around to look at me.

Aaron shifted on the couch seat. "Nevaeh, you seem to have brought some of your... stuff. Why'd you do that? And how much did you bring?"

Now it sounded like he was interviewing me. Which, in a way, I suppose they were. A house-mate interview.

"I... brought everything I need. As to why..." I took a deep breath, "God, this is harder than I thought it would be."

"Nothing good is easy," Grayson said, his tone that of a man who could lead the masses. Strong and stable.

"True... okay." I pulled myself up to sit up straight. "I brought everything here, because I was hoping that your feelings about me hadn't changed. That you still want me to live with you. So... I brought everything I need to move in, if you'll have me?"

"If we still want you? Nothing's changed here. Why would it?" Grayson asked.

I threw up my hands. "I don't know! Because you're mad at me and hardly speaking to me anymore? Because I ran away and you didn't follow. You didn't call, or anything. But then, when Trevor came to attack me, you knew... So, I don't really know what to think now."

Grayson continued to stare at me with those eyes that pierced my soul. "Well, we haven't changed our minds about how much we want you. If anything, after yesterday, a part of me wants to lock you in the bedroom so no one ever hurts you again."

I hiccupped out a laugh. "I sort of understand that."

Because I felt the same way, especially about Brad. Maybe we could come to an arrangement where none of us would put anyone into a dangerous situation ever again.

Brad was grinning like a loon. "So, you're moving in. You're here to stay? You want to be our mate?"

I nodded. "I do. I can't promise I'll always totally get all this..." I gestured to the house and them. "But I'll try my best because I don't want to live without you."

They'd sacrificed themselves for me. They wanted me above all others. What more could I possibly want?

Grayson stood and I swallowed hard.

Decision time.

I looked up at him, not daring to blink in case I missed something.

"Nevaeh, we love you," Grayson said. "Our bond demands us to give you all that we are, and more. But you left us, rejected our lovemaking and all our gifts."

I nodded and hot tears slid down my cheeks, emotion clogging my throat.

I wanted to deny it, but it was time to grow up and be accountable for my outbursts and actions. "Yes, I did. I was scared. And I am so sorry for hurting you all."

Grayson nodded, seemingly waiting for more. My gaze dropped down his body. Worshipping at the altar of Grayson was the best way forward. I knew that. But to put myself out there, only to be rejected, would be my worst nightmare come true.

I fell to my knees. These men had quite literally taken a bullet for me. If they rejected me now, I could take it. I could.

I dropped onto all fours and crawled over to him.

Yes, I crawled.

While I was unpacking, Claire had explained some things about the Alphas. They were truly dominant by nature. Not assholes, but leaders, who needed the respect of their family and those who followed them. The best way to show them that was to submit. And Claire promised me that if I did that, truly did that, then my life would never be better.

"You showed me how amazing lovemaking could be. And I

promise you, I'll never run from it again. No matter how scarily beautiful it is."

I rested on my heels when I reached his feet, and sat looking up, though my gaze kept catching on the bulge behind his zipper.

Grayson's arms fell to his sides, and he stared down at me. "What are you doing, little one?" His tone had changed.

He wasn't angry anymore. He was aroused. He swallowed, his throat working hard.

"I'm waiting for you to tell me I can suck your cock."

The words came out of my mouth as though I were a person standing on the ceiling looking down. I had no control over what I just said.

Shit.

"I don't need to give you permission," he said, a slow grin warming his expression. "After the other day, I think it would be better if you took what you wanted, Nevaeh. Actions speak louder than words, after all. So, I'll know you really want it."

Happiness swelled in my heart as I looked up at him and realized how much he loved me. He was forgiving me for hurting him, and Aaron, and Brad. And that's all I wanted. To start over again.

I went up on my knees, and with trembling hands, reached for his jeans. I undid the button and slowly pulled down the zipper, tooth by tooth. Bushy hair was my surprise, no underwear to be found. I pulled the jeans apart and tugged them down until his cock bounced up at me, already thick, hard and wanting.

I hummed happily as I wrapped my hand around the impressive shaft and put the head into my mouth. He was salty and hot and beautiful.

He grabbed my hair and held my head, thrusting his hips gently as gasps and moans filled the air. I took as much of him as I could, saliva accumulating until I had to pull off.

He backed away and I cried out, "No."

The rejection kicked me in the guts.

He chuckled and landed on the couch with a thump. "Oh, sweetheart, there will be more later, but I think Aaron deserves an apology too."

Aaron walked over and I looked up at him, keeping my face as sincere as possible so he knew I was serious.

"I'm sorry for hurting you the other day. I promise I won't do that again."

"You won't what? Fuck me and then leave me?" His tone was hurt and I nodded, realizing that before me were three very different men. And I would have to learn over time what each of them needed from me.

"No. Never again." What else could I say?

"Then ask me," he said, and for the first time I was lost.

"Ah... Ask you what?"

He gestured down and I grinned. Oh, yes, definitely. "Aaron... May I please suck your cock?"

He nodded but didn't move, and I attacked him more fiercely than I had with Grayson, maintaining eye contact the whole time as I took out his flesh and began stroking him.

He was still upset; I could feel it.

"Can I do anything else for you, Aaron? I really do want to stay with you... be here for you. Do you want me to quit my work for you guys?"

That was the last thing I wanted, but if that's what it took, I would consider it. I hoped that if they loved me, they wouldn't ask me to do that. But I would if that's what it took to make things right with these three men.

My mates.

"You'd do that for us?" he asked, stroking my cheek.

I nodded and pressed a kiss to the head of his cock, warm and pulsing in my hand. "I'd do anything for you." And I would. They deserved my loyalty and love.

"Thank you," he said and pushed my head down.

I slid his cock into my mouth, my mind spinning. Did that mean he wanted me to stop working? I pushed the fear down. Did it really matter? All I'd ever dreamed of was a house I could call my own, a home, and a partner to love me.

I'd gotten far more than that.

The rest was all superficial shit that I could let go of. I could.

16

NEVAEH

*A*aron tugged at my hair when I applied extra suction and staggered back too. "Whoa... you're too good at that."

He was holding his cock tightly, like he was trying to stop an impending orgasm. "Ah... thanks."

No one had ever told me that, and I glowed with the compliment. I wanted to be good at it. I wanted to be good at everything. I never wanted them to want or crave for another woman.

"And just so you know," Aaron continued, "I'd never take your job away from you. It's handy having a nurse in the family." He grinned at me.

My heart broke and was remade in that instant.

I gave him my biggest smile and put all my love into the words as I said, "Thank you."

But I had one more to go. I stood and walked over to the man who'd taken gunfire for me. Brad was still sitting in his allocated spot on the couch. But as I approached, he pushed his jeans down and opened his zipper for me.

"Can I suck your cock, Brad? Pretty please?"

He laughed and nodded. "Yeah, get down here."

With Brad, I knew it was more a token gesture than anything else. He had already forgiven me.

I moved to kneel on the couch so I could dive into his lap, when Grayson grabbed my shoulder. "Strip."

"But I..." Needed to do Brad.

"Yes. Strip, then get to Brad."

"Okay." In the bright light of the lounge room? Sure. Why not?

I took off my tank and bra, letting my small boobs free of their confines. Next was my pants. I hated my legs. Too thin, some people said, yet all I could see were fatty lumps everywhere.

But this wasn't about me, it was about making them feel loved. So, I pushed through the incredible amount of discomfort I felt and heard the loud groan behind me.

"Fuck, woman. I almost came just from looking at you. You are too bloody hot." That was Aaron, and as I looked over at Grayson, he growled and shook his head.

I glanced at Brad. "Is he okay?"

Brad laughed. "Oh, yeah. He's battling his shifter because his wolf wants you as much as his human half does. Come suck me, and he'll pull himself together."

I bit my lip and glanced back over at the Alpha. I didn't understand. Was he mad at me?

Brad squeezed my hand. "Hey, this is a massive compliment, Nevaeh. Grayson is the most controlled Alpha in our whole pack, and you are his undoing."

He grinned and tugged at me.

When I looked over my shoulder at Grayson once more, he was stroking his cock and groaning, lust and need evident in his eyes.

Okay... I can do this.

The energy had changed in the room. It was heavy and hot. I

knelt on the couch and put my lips around Brad's cock. He put his hand on my head and I sucked on his flesh.

I moaned and tongued the saltiness, loving the feel of him in my mouth. Then suddenly, hands grabbed my thighs and a tongue thrust between my legs.

I released Brad's cock from my mouth at the shock. "Oh my God!" I screamed out as, I assumed it was Aaron, ran his tongue over all my aching parts.

Brad tugged on my head and I went down on him again, feeling his cock hard and large in my mouth.

Aaron slid his tongue inside me and I cried out, the sounds muffled by Brad's cock. He moved to my clit, flicking it from side to side. God, it felt amazing!

And then he was gone and my flesh throbbed. Needing, wanting.

No, come back!

Then Aaron was grabbing my hips and filling my pussy with his cock. I moaned and came off Brad's cock to pant and cry out. "That feels so good!"

I looked over my shoulder to confirm what I already knew. From his hands, from his technique—it was Aaron—taking me hard and fast.

I couldn't concentrate, couldn't give to Brad. I could only feel how incredible it was to have Aaron's cock back inside of me. "I missed you... Oh... damn, I missed this... Oh... fuck."

I was going to come. My belly was too tight, my pleasure balancing on a precipice of feeling. Aaron pounded into me, harder and harder, pushing me over the edge and making me scream out as the pleasure overtook me.

He came with me, his roar of completion making me close my eyes and soak up every second of this moment with him. It went on and on, the stars of orgasmic pleasure bursting inside my mind as my body shivered and shook.

Aaron pulled out and I fell forward.

Brad caught me and arranged me over his lap. His lips were on my face, in my hair, whispering to me. "You are so beautiful. Tell me when you're ready to ride me, because I am dying to be inside you again."

As though his words had inspired the hunger, my belly squeezed and tightened in response. I pushed back my hair and lifted myself up and threw my leg over his lap, over his cock.

Brad stared into my eyes, the depth of the brown irises making me ache inside my chest, where my heart was bursting with love.

He grabbed my hips and pulled me down. His cock slid inside me, impaling me and splitting me in half. I gasped as he captured my mouth in a kiss to end all kisses. It went on and on. My beautiful, passionate Omega, Brad.

I threw myself right into him, the way I threw myself beneath a wave at the ocean. With vigor, passion, and abandon. I rode him hard and fast, rolling my hips and taking him inside my body again and again. I sucked on his tongue and clung to his neck until he pulled me down on him, hard, and the ripples of his orgasm pulsed inside me. I opened my eyes and saw the pleasure flicker across his face. I kissed his lips over and over again, absorbing the love and acceptance, and beauty that I felt.

Brad smiled and sighed, letting his body relax into the bliss. I'd had two of them and yet I knew there was more to come.

My skin tingled with need.

I looked around and found the Alpha waiting. Sitting on a chair with his jeans open and an intense look on his face I couldn't read. I kissed Brad and stood up, careful not to hurt his leg any more than I already had.

I walked across the room slowly, the wetness between my thighs a reminder of everything I'd just done. And that I would continue to do. "You waited until last again. Why?"

I had to know.

Grayson seemed to be the most selfless man, but was that really possible? For a man to be so wonderful?

He shrugged. "The pack's needs are more important than mine."

"Do you really believe that?"

He nodded, and for the first time in my life, I knew I'd met a true Alpha. A real leader. A man who would move mountains for his people, and it gave me an incredible amount of security and hope to know that I would benefit from that love and possessive streak.

"Am I part of your pack, Grayson?"

He nodded. "If you want to be."

"I do...very much. What do I have to do, to join?"

I couldn't believe I was having this conversation, fully naked, in the lounge room, the smell of sex thick in the air. But Grayson needed this, the words. I could tell.

His mouth flattened. "There are no strings attached, Nevaeh."

I knelt in front of him like I had before, showing my submission, trying to show with actions, and not just words, that I wanted to please him.

"I mean... What do you desire, Grayson? For me to be your perfect mate, tell me what I need to do."

He growled, a low, dangerous noise that made my pussy clench with want and my heart race to a new, invigorated beat.

"Tell me," I whispered again.

"Stand up," he said.

I did, shooting to my feet.

He stood also and dropped his jeans to the ground. His cock wasn't fully erect yet, but it was thickening before my very eyes. Rising to point toward me. It was hypnotic and I struggled not to stare.

"You'll be loyal," Grayson began.

"Yes." I nodded.

"You'll love us and be faithful to us."

"Yes." I nodded again. That was a given.

He began to walk forward and pushed me back until my spine hit the wall and he was staring down at me.

"Open your legs," he said, and I did, eagerly.

I was panting now, desperate to find out what he would do next. I spread my legs as wide as I could while standing, and he slid his hand between my thighs. His fingertips moved over my clit and around my opening, spreading the juices while I gasped and moaned.

"You will be honest with us, and scream at us, and fight with us, and moan at our touch, and fuck us, but you will not run away from us. Never again." He thrust a long finger up inside my pussy and I screamed, the possessive presence inside my body making a statement.

I nodded again and again as he spoke, my eyelids too heavy to keep open as he worked my body with perfect precision. His finger slid over my g-spot and pleasure swept through my belly. My knees buckled and he leaned against me to hold me up.

"Say it. Say you won't leave us again."

Tears gathered in my eyes, but I forced them to open. "I won't leave again, I promise. If you promise you'll never leave me."

Grayson growled and removed his fingers. I gasped at the loss, but as he grabbed my waist and lifted me, I knew I'd soon be full again.

Grayson pinned me to the wall with his huge body. I was helpless and I loved it. Because if I knew anything in this weird, crazy world, it was that this man loved me. And that he'd never hurt me.

He impaled me on his massive cock in one strong move. I groaned and squeezed him tightly. "Tell me, Grayson... please."

He reached under my ass and held me tight, moving in and out of me with measured thrusts. "I'll never leave you. I'd die for you. I'll tear apart that bear next time I see him."

I gasped and grabbed for his back, scratching at his skin as I ached to get closer.

Grayson set his lips to my ear and I wrapped my legs and arms around him, pulling him as close as I could. "Will you give me babies, Nevaeh? Will you birth our child from this perfect body of yours?"

I nodded and squeezed my eyes shut as my love spilled over and the tears flowed down my face.

"Say it," he demanded, and I nodded again.

He began to fuck me harder, faster, like he'd force the confession from my soul. *A baby... a true link.* Something I'd been terrified of my whole life—connecting myself so wholly to a person.

"Yes," I whispered. The tears streamed down my face as my belly began to squeeze and tighten.

"Say it again," he demanded, grabbing my ass even tighter.

"Yes," I said, this time louder. I held him to me, welcoming his cock into the deep recesses of my body, my soul, where I'd grow him a son.

Or a daughter.

Or both.

"Yes. I want your babies. I'll give you anything you want if you'll only love me forever."

His laugh mixed with his growl. "Deal."

He fucked me into the wall, our bodies heaving against one another, straining until our orgasms mixed together. My body milked him of the seed that would grow the babies who would bind us together for life.

EPILOGUE

GRAYSON

Nine months later

I drove home from Little River, my car full of the thousands of things Nevaeh had requested for the arrival of our baby. All the things she wanted in the house before they were born. Diapers and blankets, a cot and a car seat. Not to mention bottles, pacifiers, scales and a new bath.

Phew.

I pulled up behind the back of the house and sat for a while. So much had changed in so little time. I was stronger and more assertive than I'd ever been, and our family was flourishing.

I grabbed some bags from the passenger seat and went to open the door when I saw her. *My mate.* Waddling over to Claire's house and knocking on her door. She leaned back over a hand pressed into her spine, her massive belly protruding forward.

Nevaeh had been a dream come true, in every sense of the word.

She was hardworking and tough, but super sweet and sexy as

hell. She completed our pack, and I liked to think that we completed her, as well.

Nevaeh entered Claire's house and I got out of the car, carrying all the bags into our home and then coming back for the boxes.

So much stuff... and we didn't even know how many we were having.

Nevaeh had refused the ultrasound that Claire had offered. She was superstitious, and terrified that things would go wrong.

It had been such a strange nine months in that way. Nevaeh had turned from a beautiful young mate who barely had her footing in this world, to a terrified, and yet super-obstinate mama wolf.

Once I'd unpacked everything and Nevaeh still hadn't returned from Claire's, I decided to go visit my neighbors.

A slither of excitement coursed through my blood. It happened every single time I knew I was about to see my mate. It was a great feeling. And it still made me thank God every single night for the gift that was my Heaven.

I knocked on the door and waited. Even after all this time, I liked to wait for Claire to open the door before barging in. Dexter was still obsessed by her and their children, and he'd take my head off if I stepped out of line.

A smile lifted my lips. Or he'd try, anyway. I was stronger and faster than I'd ever been, thanks to my mate's love and all the sex we had. Though...thanks to Claire, Dex would be a close second in strength.

The door swung open and Claire was before me, a worried look on her face.

"What's wrong?" I asked.

"Um... your mate's in labor."

A grin stretched my lips. It was a few weeks early, but I believed that was still okay. "Great. Where is she?"

"This way."

Claire directed me up the stairs to the bathroom, where Nevaeh was standing in the shower, naked and moaning softly, her eyes closed. "Sweetheart, are you okay?"

She didn't look okay.

"Um... I don't know."

She began to groan louder, her head hanging forward as she leaned against the wall with her hands outstretched on the cold tiles.

I turned to Claire. "What's going on, Claire?"

"Nevaeh's in the late stages of labor. She's been having contractions all last night and today but didn't tell anyone. She should go to the hospital, but she doesn't want to."

"No..." Nevaeh shook her head, "I don't know... what... they'll be."

Claire reached out and ran her hand down Nevaeh's back. "Your babies will be like mine. Healthy and human, Nevaeh."

Nevaeh turned suddenly and grabbed Claire's hand, her huge, swollen belly rippling under the stream of hot water.

"No. I have you. That's all I need. Please, Claire... please... I..." She broke off to groan and I turned away.

I needed to find Aaron and Brad. "Sweetheart, shall I get the others?"

Nevaeh nodded but didn't seem able to speak.

I turned to Claire. "What do I do?"

She smiled. "I have everything we need. I brought it all here from the hospital when my babies were born. I'll stay here with Nevaeh. You go get your pack."

"Okay."

I stepped into the shower and kissed Nevaeh quickly on the side of her face. "I won't be long, beautiful."

I turned to leave, but Claire grabbed me. "Hurry. It won't be long now."

My heart jumped. I nodded and ran. I found Brad at his parents' place, and Aaron at one of the clothing shops, buying something for Nevaeh. I'd never been so grateful that the town was so small. "Quick. We've gotta go."

They didn't question me, they just followed. By the time we got back to Claire's house, Dex and the boys were camped in the lounge.

"Is she..." There was moaning from upstairs and we bolted up to the second floor.

Nevaeh was still in the shower, but she was kneeling down on the tiles, some sort of thin padding beneath her.

"You're doing so well, Nevaeh. Just push, gently. Slowly."

Over the next twenty minutes, I watched a miracle occur. My perfect, healthy mate gave birth to not one, not two, but three babies. All girls. All perfect.

When Claire had given birth to the first daughter in three decades, there had been a town wide party that had lasted three days. With our girls now born, here and well, the packs truly had something to celebrate! The curse was broken.

I held one tiny babe, and my pack mates held the others. I could have cried, if my heart wasn't so full of love and happiness. Claire took them from us, one by one, and tied off their cords and wrapped them in blankets before handing our daughters back to us.

"Come on, Mom, bed's this way," Claire said.

She helped Nevaeh to her feet and dried her body. Nevaeh was flushed and still sweaty, despite the shower. She'd never looked more beautiful.

We all climbed onto the bed Claire told us to rest in, crowding around our mate and laying her babies on her body. "You did it, beautiful."

She grinned up at us, her face alight with wonder. "I did. God, that was intense. Are you sure they're all okay?"

She looked from one to the other, their perfect little faces screwed up as they mewled like kittens.

"Yes. Claire said they're perfect," Aaron said. "And they are. Just like their mother."

Nevaeh rearranged one of the girls to take a nipple and the hungry little one latched on quickly.

"She's going to be trouble, I can tell already," Brad laughed.

"Three daughters?" I coughed. "I'm buying a shotgun."

We all laughed, and I pressed a gentle kiss to my mate's lips. Nevaeh was a miracle, as were our babies. And I now had more lives to protect and love. A perfect pack. My Alpha's calling.

Life had never been so perfect.

THE END of book 2.

Book 3 in the Woodland Pack's series, 'Saving the Pack' is available now.

Download and read:
https://books2read.com/u/bxa66P

Or read on for a sneak peek.

1

CELESTE

I was going to be sick, and the toilet was too far away. I ran as fast as I could, knocking my knee painfully against the water closet door frame as I rushed into the tiny room. "Ow!"

The heat rushed up my throat and I grabbed for my hair, holding it out of the way as I launched my body forward.

"Bleh...."

The acidic bile rushed up my throat and into the toilet bowl, splashing against the sides and making me retch and choke. The smell burnt my nose and tears rolled down my cheeks, until finally, mercifully, it stopped.

I reached for the thin toilet paper beside me, pulling it from the roll, and dabbing at my mouth. I swallowed hard, though my mouth was too dry. *Yuck.*

"Oh... dear God." That was terrible.

And it hadn't stopped yet.

Every day I'd been sick. Every morning, to be precise. Until about lunchtime. For two weeks. I couldn't ignore the truth any longer.

"I'm in trouble here."

The front door to the apartment banged open and I jumped onto the toilet seat, my head spinning with fatigue and low blood pressure.

"Celeste!"

I pushed the door quickly shut and pulled down my pants, so it looked like I was using the toilet for something more than vomiting. In case he came in. Like he had in the past.

There was no such thing as privacy if you were a member of the Little Rock bear's den. I called out to him. "In the toilet. I'll be out soon."

The bile rose again. Oh, no. My gut churned and tightened. But I closed my eyes and forced it down, swallowing hard against the automatic reflex to let it all out.

I couldn't let them know my secret. I couldn't. They'd never forgive me.

Loud footsteps walked up the hallway, then a fist pounded the door, hard. I jumped, shivering with cold and fear

"Hurry up! The kitchen isn't going to clean itself!"

I rolled my eyes because he couldn't see me. If anyone knew that, I did. "Um, one minute. Sorry. I'll be right out."

He grunted and walked away.

I relaxed against the commode as I heard his footsteps fade away, my whole body shaking with stress. How long was I going to be able to hide this from the den? And when they finally found out, which was inevitable, what would they do? Force me to get an abortion? Or something worse?

I exhaled in a long sigh. Time to get moving.

I opened the water closet door and moved into the small bathroom next door, splashing some cold water onto my hot cheeks. Uncle Dennis, my adoptive father's brother, was my "employer." He had me working seven days a week in a job no one else would do.

The bears owned a run-down block of apartments. Some of the floors were rented out to outsiders, the rest were occupied by members of the den, including me. And the way I paid for my tiny bedroom in this apartment I shared with four others was to clean every bathroom in the block.

All forty-six of them.

I exhaled slowly, garnering whatever self-preserving courage I had.

Just one step at a time. You can do this.

I walked to the old kitchen and grabbed some saltine crackers from the cupboard, crunching on the only thing that kept the nausea at bay. I took a moment to breathe and get some food into my belly, then I got to work.

Of course, it wasn't just my job to clean every bathroom in the block of apartments. It was also my delight to clean the kitchen and the entire apartment I slept in. Even though five of us lived there.

My nose burned with a sudden foul smell and my throat convulsed. *Oh, no.* Then the front door flew open and three, burly, bear-shifting men walked in.

Great. My uncle was back, and with two of the others who'd shunned me when they found out I was human.

And the smell of them.... Oh my God. I couldn't hold it in. I rushed to the newly cleaned kitchen sink. My back heaved as my stomach emptied the contents I'd managed to get into it.

"What's going on with you? You sick again?" The voice was angry, annoyed. Like it always was with me. Or had been, since I reached maturity and the bears had decided I was unworthy of a mate.

Not a single man had wanted me. Despite all my hopes and dreams of a real family, I'd been rejected. Wholeheartedly.

I nodded and rinsed out my mouth. "Ah, yeah... sorry. I'll get back to cleaning."

I kept my head down, attempting to walk around the three man-mountains in the kitchen. Each smelled as bad as the other.

"Stop." The command in my uncle's voice made me freeze. Or as close as I could, considering I was shivering like a leaf in autumn.

"What..." My uncle bent down and smelled me, sniffing loudly. "You smell even worse than normal. Almost like a.... wolf."

My eyes fell shut as my stomach dropped to my feet. They knew. They knew, and they would punish me for my mistake. Rough hands grabbed my chin and forced my head up. Uncle Dennis' eyes bored down on me.

"Tell me. Now."

"What... I mean... Tell you?" I was stammering, I was so scared. My arms and legs shook. Goosebumps covered my skin.

"Lou, Davie, come here and smell her. Tell me if you smell what I do?"

Oh, God, no!

I kept my arms pinned to my sides and didn't breathe. This was the most humiliating thing about being part of this family. They all said I smelled weird. Worse than weird. Bad. Disgusting.

Or that's what the bears said.

So, I scrubbed myself clean three times a day, even taking betadine into the shower some days to disinfect myself. It hadn't changed anything. They still hated me.

"She's knocked up," Lou grunted.

"Yeah, but by who?" Uncle Dennis growled.

He wrapped a hand around my throat and forced me back until my spine touched the wall and I gasped for air. *No!* I grabbed his hands and pulled on them, the pain making my head spin. I couldn't breathe.

Oh God...

"None of us wanted you, it can't be a bear's baby. So, who was it, you little slut?"

I couldn't lie, I had to tell them the truth. I'd been lonely and desperate, and he'd made me feel more loved in a single hour than I'd experienced my whole life.

"Just… a guy. In town. At a bar."

Uncle Dennis dropped me to the ground. I inhaled quickly, needing the air. I stayed where he'd left me, on my hands and knees. I wasn't getting back up just to be knocked down again. I'd learnt that lesson the hardest way.

As one of the only non-shifting women in the whole den, I was the weakest by far. I had the scars and the broken bones to prove it.

"It smells like a wolf," he growled above me.

I kept my head down. They weren't talking to me.

"We always knew she smelled like them," Uncle Dennis said.

"One of their human mates." Lou spat.

What? I listened intently, though I tried not to show how interested I was. A wolf's Fated Mate? How was that possible? I was human.

"You know the Alpha doesn't want the wolves getting any more of them," Lou growled, and I heard Uncle Dennis' sigh.

Any more of them? Of what? Humans? Mates?

"Let's take her to the Alpha and find out what he wants to do with her."

They hoisted me to my feet, and I went with them willingly. Being submissive to the bears had kept me alive and relatively well fed.

I relaxed as much as I could, an unnatural calm descending over me. I'd known this day would come, sooner or later. They'd realize I wasn't suited for their Den, and they'd either kick me out, or ship me off.

But now that the worst had finally arrived, I was calm. My

mind worked faster than it ever had. There was more than me at stake now. My baby needed protection from the men who towered over us.

There was only one thing to do. When I got the chance, I'd run. And thanks to Lou spilling the beans about my wolf-like smell, I knew where to go for refuge. Tayte, the Alpha wolf-shifter had said something strange the night we'd met.

About a woman, a doctor, who was the first human mate they'd found in town. I'd memorized that piece of information somehow through my alcohol fogged brain.

My baby and I needed protection, and the Daddy wolf who gave me this baby was the only one who could give it to me.

DEATH! *They'd sentenced me to death!*

The family that had taken me in as a baby, raised me. Whom I'd slaved for. Whom I'd tried to love to the best of my ability. I'd spent years caring for their children... and this was the result?

They'd all turned their backs on me.

With a single word from the new Alpha, Trevor, they decided I needed to die. I still couldn't believe it. So, I decided to escape, of course. What choice did I have?

They'd chosen to kill me in the morning, when they had time, so to speak. Idiots. They hadn't even bothered to chain me up.

They'd locked me in my room, but probably assumed I wouldn't try to get away. That I'd just do as I was told and fall in with their plans, like I always did.

Not this time. Not when my life, and my baby's life, was on the line.

As soon as they were all asleep, I managed to break out of my locked bedroom. I'd done it before. It wasn't difficult with the old locks.

I crept through the apartment, avoiding the creaking wood panels I knew by heart, and ran. Through the exit stairwell, down the many flights of stairs and out into the cold night air.

I didn't even stop to shiver in the tank top and thin jeans I wore, I just started running. Through the city, heading for the hospital. Towards the woman who could help me.

God... please.

We were as far away from the inner city as you could get, but the streetlights lit my path, showing me the way to safety.

My heart galloped in my chest.

My throat burned as I gasped in and out.

If the bears realized I was gone, they would chase me, and I'd be done for. I had no protection, no weapon. The only thing I had were my two legs and the will of a mother fighting for her child's life.

It had to be enough. I kept running, city block after city block, though my tired, starving body screamed at me to stop. Adrenaline pumped harder and I increased my pace, turning the corners as quickly as I could.

The streets were deserted. It had to be past two am. I didn't really know. I kept going, pausing to breathe at an intersection to get my bearings, my chest heaving with exertion.

Which way?

They didn't let me out very much and I wasn't very familiar with the street signs, though I'd lived here all my life.

I looked and looked, then saw a sign I recognized.

Yes! The supermarket. It wasn't far from the hospital.

Keep going.

I pushed off again, my legs screaming at me for those first few steps until I found my rhythm once more. The hospital, safety, was about six blocks now. My thigh muscles burned as I tripped on some uneven pavement, but I kept running.

The night was silent, except for my ragged breathing, but I

could only imagine what would happen if the bears woke to find me gone. The growling and screams of terror that would follow. I knew their tempers, their fighting and hunting abilities.

I'd watched them my whole life. And if I became the hunted, rather than the observer, then I was as good as dead. Unless I could find her.

Claire. The doctor.

I turned the corner past the supermarket and ground to a halt. Suddenly, there it was. A huge, white building with bright lights and doors that opened automatically.

I staggered the last hundred feet, my energy depleted and my body relaxing as my safe haven was finally in sight. I stopped on the sidewalk, fear skittling through me.

The bears would be able to track me if I went inside the hospital right now. They'd already tracked Claire there once. I had to throw them off the scent.

Damn it.

I staggered to the right, going another block down, though fear truly raced along my nerves now. I ripped off my tank and dropped on a park bench. I walked to the next one and took off my jeans.

"Oh my God."

It was freaking freezing!! I jumped up and down in my old underwear and then ran back to the hospital. Hopefully that would help!

I ran straight into the Emergency Room and the bright lights enveloped me. I was shaking, freezing, panting and half naked. The nurses rushed at me from everywhere. With blankets and juice, and nice words.

They admitted me straight away. "What's happened dear, were you attacked? Shall we call the police?"

The old nurse was preparing a bag of fluid and as she came for me, needle ready to put in my arm. I stopped her.

"Can I please have a shower? I smell bad, and I'm so cold."

My scent would be greatly reduced after a shower. And thanks to the bears grabbing me early yesterday, I hadn't had one in over twenty-four hours.

"Of course, you can, after we've done a few tests."

I stood up. I couldn't let her win this one. "No please. It's important. I'm pregnant and I need to see Claire."

"Claire?" The nurse blinked and put the needle down. "She's not working tonight but I may have someone else who could help you."

I shuffled towards the shower room. "Please. I just need two minutes in the shower, then you can test me as much as you like."

The nurse nodded and I jumped into the shower, scrubbing my trembling body with the sterile smelling soap and even washing my hair. Someone had left some shampoo in the stall, and I couldn't resist. I didn't get the luxury much at home.

"Here you go." Someone stuck her arm into the cubicle and offered me a fresh white towel.

I turned the water off and reached for the towel. "Oh, that's heavenly! Thank you."

The person behind the door laughed.

"What's funny?" I asked, frowning at her, though she couldn't see me.

Surely the fact that a hospital towel was the cleanest piece of linen I'd seen in my whole life wasn't to be laughed at.

"I'll explain in a sec. I was told you came in with no clothes. I had some spare yoga pants and a jumper in my locker."

She placed the bag inside the bathroom, then shut the door again.

Tears pricked in my nose and I blinked them back. "That's... ah ... so kind of you."

I quickly dried my body and wrapped my wet hair up with the towel. The yoga pants were the perfect size, though a little tight around my tummy, and the jumper was snuggly and warm, though way too big.

How tall was this woman? I glanced at my reflection in the mirror. I was red and blotchy, but clean and safe. I'd take it.

When I stepped out of the bathroom there was a young nurse sitting on the bed. She grinned at me with a lazy confidence I'd only seen in the extremely powerful shifters in my den.

All men.

"Um... I'm Celeste."

She grinned. "Nevaeh."

"Nevaeh..." I'd never heard of it.

"That's why I laughed before. You said, heavenly. My name is heaven spelled backwards."

I stared at her, wondering if she was joking.

She laughed. "It's true. I used to hate it, but since meeting my guys, I don't stress anymore."

Had she just said "Guys?" As in, more than one?

She didn't answer my question though, instead she pulled her cell phone from her pocket.

"I know you wanted to see Claire, but she's at home. She's pregnant and working less hours. Why did you ask for her?" Nevaeh's tone was casual, but I had a feeling she knew why I was here.

"Ah... that's great about her being pregnant."

Maybe I shouldn't have come here? I didn't know these people. How could I trust them?

This was a stupid idea. I edged towards the door. "Um... I think I'll get going."

Nevaeh stood up. "Hey, don't freak out. You're pregnant too?"

I hesitated, then realized I'd told the first nurse the truth. So, I nodded.

Nevaeh moved around the room and gestured to the bed.

"I'm not going to hurt you, I promise. Have a seat and I'll explain."

I had pretty good instincts when it came to evil intent and as I reached out with those senses, I came up with nothing.

Hmmm... okay.

I walked back to the small bed, climbed onto the thin mattress and pulled the blanket over me. It was so nice to be warm.

Nevaeh stepped towards me slowly. "Mind if I put the drip in now that you've showered?"

I nodded. "Sure."

Not for me, but for the baby you can.

I rolled up my sleeve and she walked across to me, sliding the needle into my hand effortlessly and then taping it down.

Wow. She's good at that.

"You need your fluids," she said as though that explained everything, then sat again in her chair. "Look, Celeste, I'm willing to tell you everything about me and Claire, but you have to show me that you need to know. If you know what I mean?"

She smiled and waited. I got the drift and sighed.

What did I have to lose at this point?

"I lived with the bear shifters just out of town. But they found out yesterday that I'm pregnant and they want to kill me. So, I ran."

Nevaeh slid to the edge of her chair. "Holy shit."

"Yeah."

Then she snorted. "Sounds like me last month."

Sorry? "Ah... what?"

Nevaeh shrugged and met my gaze. "I'm not sure if you heard, but I'm the female that Trevor was stalking."

She was *the girl?* My gaze ran over the woman in front of me. Tall, thin and super pretty. "You're the one who killed our Alpha."

I was shocked. I'd expected someone so much bigger, stronger, more shifter-like.

Nevaeh nodded. "Unfortunately, yes that's me. He was trying to kill my mates."

She looked a bit regretful, but not very sorry. And I didn't blame her, if what she said was true.

"Trevor's our Alpha now. I never much liked his father."

I slammed a hand over my mouth. I couldn't believe I'd actually said it!

Such a comment would have normally gotten me whipped.

Nevaeh winced. "I wish I'd gotten him, too. Bastard." Then her gaze zeroed in on me.

"So, why are you here, Celeste? You obviously know about the shifting world. And you're running from the bears. How can Claire and I help you? And how did you know to come here for her, anyway?"

I licked my dry lips and Nevaeh handed me a bottle of water. I smiled with gratitude. She was being so nice to me. I needed to be honest with her. "I heard about Claire from Tayte, a guy I met in a bar a couple of months ago. He told me about his town, and how Claire was the first mate they'd found in years."

Nevaeh's eyes opened even wider. "Tayte told you about the pack? About Claire?"

She looked surprised, and a bit upset.

I jumped in to defend him. They probably weren't allowed to tell humans about their world. "Yeah. He could smell the bears on me, so he knew I lived with them. And he was pretty drunk... so was I. I'm not sure he meant to tell me so much, but don't worry, I never said anything to any of the bears about her. They knew anyway, somehow. That the wolves had found their first mate. That's why they tried to keep you away. Wait a minute."

All the pieces suddenly clicked into place. "You're a wolf mate too!"

Her lips stretched up into a huge smile. "Yes, I am. But do you mean too, as in like Claire... or do you mean too... as in like you?"

She raised her eyebrows, and my hands flew to my still flat stomach. I didn't want to answer that, and if I were honest, I didn't really know. I was going on the word of bears. What would they know about wolf Fated Mates?

"Is Tayte the father?" Nevaeh asked quietly.

I waited a heartbeat, then told the truth. "Yes, that's why I came here. To find Claire. To ask for her help in getting to the pack. I know I come with a whole lot of trouble at my back, but I need to find Tayte and see if he can protect me and the baby."

Nevaeh began pressing buttons on her cell phone.

"Who are you calling? It's probably three in the morning."

Nevaeh put the phone to her ear and gestured for me not to stress with a flutter of her hands. "Trust me, Grayson's gonna wanna hear this."

~

Continue reading:
https://books2read.com/u/bxa66P